A DUKE FOR LADY EVE

ALSO BY KASEY STOCKTON

Women of Worth Series

Love in the Bargain

Love for the Spinster

Love at the House Party

Love in the Wager

Love in the Ballroom

Ladies of Devon

The Jewels of Halstead Manor

The Lady of Larkspur Vale

Stand-alone Historical Romance

His Amiable Bride

A Forgiving Heart

❅

Contemporary Romance

Snowflake Wishes

His Stand-In Holiday Girlfriend

Snowed In on Main Street

A Duke for Lady Eve

Kasey Stockton

Golden Owl Press

This is a work of fiction. Names, characters, places, and incidents either are the product of the author's imagination or are used fictitiously. Any resemblance to actual persons, living or dead, events, or locales is entirely coincidental.

Copyright © 2019 by Kasey Stockton
Cover design by Ashtyn Newbold

First print edition: November 2019
All rights reserved. No part of this book may be reproduced or used in any manner without written permission of the copyright owner except for the use of quotations for the purpose of a book review.

For everyone who plans to curl up with a book under the light of a Christmas tree. Happy reading & Merry Christmas.

CHAPTER 1

LONDON, 1813

*F*rom her vantage point behind her aunt's large, imposing feather, Evelyn Trainor could perfectly see the beautiful lace-trimmed and expertly trussed ladies lining up across from their dancing partners in the center of the room. The gentlemen were largely blocked by the ostrich's contribution to Aunt Edith's head piece. But the gentlemen were not imperative to Evelyn's current daydream—or, was it an *evening* dream—because they were not the high-society debutantes whom Evelyn wished, with each fiber of her being, she had been born to be.

"Evelyn," Aunt Edith hissed, drawing her attention away from the well-bred women beginning to dance. "Scratch just below my shoulder bone."

Obediently, Evelyn reached forward to the space between her aunt and the chair's back.

"Discreetly," Aunt Edith whispered.

How was Evelyn meant to manage that? Slowly, she began to scratch under her aunt's shoulder bone as she inched closer to the old woman's chair. Her sight was drawn back to the floor of graceful dancers and it was all too easy to imagine herself there among the ornately costumed women as though she belonged.

Glancing down, she huffed an irritated breath at her own borrowed finery. It was a blessing cousin Harriet had married and left behind her outdated gowns or Evelyn would have been forced to arrive at Lord Trenton's ball in a walking dress of puce wool. And Harriet's old costume, designed to resemble a fox, was entirely more appropriate for this masquerade.

"Evelyn, enough," Aunt Edith snapped.

Evelyn pulled back her hand, tucking it into the fold of her gown, her cheeks growing warm.

The room was not quite as full as it would have been in previous weeks. The majority of Society had returned to their country homes for Christmas weeks before the snow arrived, but Evelyn's father was determined to remain in Town until parliament disbanded and he could be sure he wouldn't miss anything. He was dedicated to his place in the House of Commons, and Evelyn did not disapprove of his passion for bettering his country.

She *did*, however, mind traveling through England in the wet, muddy snow. But alas, it could not be helped.

Fortunately for her aunt, they were able to attend one final ball before they returned to Wiltshire and Evelyn's younger brothers. Evelyn would have been happy to skip the event altogether, but it was Father's express wish that she attend as many Society functions as possible during her first—and only, if she had her way—Season. He wanted her to enjoy herself. He did not understand that Society was not Evelyn's idea of enjoyment.

"If you would step out from behind me," Aunt Edith said through clenched teeth, "you might very well be asked to dance."

Evelyn reached up and adjusted the mask over her eyes. It was a dazzling piece, fairly covered in amber and gold paste jewels with faux fox ears fastened to the top. Her maid had tied it about her head, incorporating the ribbon into her coiffure for the evening. "It is impossible to dance when I know no one here, Aunt Edith. Perhaps it would have been wiser if Lord Trenton had not insisted on a masquerade."

"Psh." Aunt Edith moved her mask away from her face with ease, waving about the stick by which it was held. Her nose wrinkled and her beady eyes took in Evelyn's own face. "It is a benefit this evening, not a hindrance. The mask covers your face well enough. Any man here would be able to imagine he was dancing with a lovely young woman."

Evelyn easily read the words her aunt had implied: *these men will dance with you because they cannot know you are plain, simple, and poor.* It was more likely Aunt Edith's austere countenance which kept the gentlemen at bay. Not that Evelyn was complaining.

"But if I danced," she said with quiet reserve, "I would not be able to keep you company, Aunt."

The old woman snorted.

Evelyn leaned back against the wall. The first dance of this set would soon come to a close. She tried not to let her imagination run away from her too dearly, but from her vantage point and with her mask covering her face, she could watch the glittering Society with unabashed interest. She couldn't help but imagine the woman she would be if she had been born to a Peer, and not a common man.

It was a game she'd been playing her entire life, and she knew it well. If she had been born to nobility, she would *clearly* be Lady Eve, instead of plain Evelyn. She would be polished, wearing nothing but light blue silk and white muslin instead of the darker, practical colors she was currently forced to wear. She would be asked to dance every dance, and—perhaps the greatest part of all—would be respected, praised, and appreciated.

"Fetch me some ratafia, Evelyn. I am parched."

The older woman's craggly, strained voice pulled Evelyn from her reverie like a swift fall from an apple tree.

It was senseless to imagine her life as Lady Eve. For it only made her reality all the more plain.

"Yes, Aunt," she said meekly. "At once."

The table where a servant stood ready to pour ratafia was only two paces from where they were stationed. It was not a far trek, but she paused before setting off, regardless. French doors which were closed to what was likely the garden in the rear of the house sat just behind the table containing the drinks.

The doors called to her, though she didn't know why. She felt overwhelmed by the people and the oppressive heat, and the cool air waiting just paces away beckoned her. It was nothing but dark beyond the square windowpanes within the doorframe; she approached them, glancing over her shoulder at the dancers and patrons, none of whom seemed to be paying her any mind.

Before she could think better of it, Evelyn opened the door and slipped outside, closing it softly behind her. The bitter, winter air seeped through her ballgown at once and she nearly turned back for the warmth of Lord Trenton's ballroom, but for a small, stone bench placed against the back hedge which immediately caught her eye. If she had been born a lady, Evelyn would have had a grand townhouse such as this one and a beautiful garden behind her house. She would have spent warm spring days sitting amidst the flowers and reading a book or drinking tea with a friend.

She would not have been tending to her brothers or worrying about her father, for they would have had funds sufficient to care for the things they stood in need of and the boys would have undoubtedly been sent to school.

Crossing the lawn, Evelyn lowered herself onto the stone bench with a huff and watched the dancers within the ballroom, much as she had earlier, though this time she felt far more removed.

Which was a more accurate description of Evelyn's life. Though they had little money, she had plenty of happiness in her home. If only Father would quit his work in the Commons and simply retire to their house in Wiltshire, then he would be well.

But asking him to quit politics and sit about the house doing nothing was akin to begging the king to step down from his throne because of a headache.

It simply would not happen.

Humming a tune she remembered her mother singing to her as a child, Evelyn watched the dancers with somber acceptance. She felt silly for dreaming so often of the lot she would have lived had she been born to a Peer, but it was nothing more than a game—a silly way to pass the time and compare her life to those who stood so far out of her reach.

And it would never be within her reach, for she would never be one of the simpering misses who stood in wait at the balls and dinners and vied for the attention of titled men. Even if she tried, said gentleman wouldn't have her anyway.

Evelyn's humming turned to a low singing. She could not be heard from within the doors, surely, for the instruments could clearly be heard outside. Her alto rang quietly through the garden. Comforted, she continued. Her voice was one of the few things that still connected her to her mother after her mother's death.

"You have a beautiful voice," a man whispered. His low, deep voice came from behind her, forcing shivers down her spine.

Jumping up, Evelyn glanced around, her breath coming in heaves. Moonlight lit the yard and cast shadows on the lawn from the candlelight in Lord Trenton's house, yet there was no one there. All that met her was a large hedge lining the back of the garden, just behind her bench. Turning in a slow circle, Evelyn squinted her eyes and raked over the small, enclosed space, but she was completely alone.

Had she imagined the man? He had sounded so close behind her, but perhaps it was all part of her dreams. Perhaps she'd imagined herself a duke.

Grinning to herself at the silliness of it all, Evelyn sat once again upon the cold stone bench and settled her hands on her lap. She knew she spent a good deal of time in her own mind. It was one of the things which had concerned her father and forced him to require she attend the Season with him this year. If only he realized that her attendance at this masquerade, and other events like it, would do very little for her social standing and pursuit of a husband.

"Please," the deep voice continued, louder this time. "Do not stop on my account."

Evelyn froze. So she hadn't imagined him after all.

Standing, Evelyn turned around and searched the thick branches of the hedge. Was this man standing somewhere within the hedge, itself?

"Might I request your name, fair maiden?"

Flowery speech was not going to sway her to disregard proper etiquette. "I am not that sort of woman, sir."

"Surely you will not deny me." His disembodied voice filtered through the branches. "I merely request an introduction, since there is no one else to do the honor on our behalf."

Shaking her head, Evelyn couldn't help but smile. Whoever this man was, two things were very clear: he was charismatic and quite used to getting his way.

His deep voice carried. "I can see you do not agree. You needn't shake your head, you know."

She stilled. He could see her. "I am at a disadvantage," Evelyn said. "You can see me, but I fear I cannot see you."

"You are not looking in the right place. Step up on that bench and you will not need to strain your eyes."

Dare she?

Pulling up her gown, Evelyn lifted one foot and settled it securely on the bench. Moments later she had her second foot up and stood looking over the hedge and into the garden of another townhouse. Oh, dear. It was an even bigger townhouse than the one she currently visited. Clearly this man was not someone of low birth or social standing.

After she was appropriately awed by his house, she glanced down and found a man standing just beyond the hedge, his serious gaze trained on her.

She paused, caught by his vision. His dark hair was tousled and his jaw unshaven, but he was otherwise well-dressed. She had been correct; he was a man of superior birth. If his clothing had not told her so alone, his bearing certainly did.

Standing tall, he bent in a distinguished bow. "Duke of Alverton, at your pleasure. Now, fair maiden, please do me the honor of telling me your name, for I must know it."

Swallowing a lump which would not allow her to speak, Evelyn faltered. He was not simply a man of high birth. He was a *duke*. Had she conjured him from her thoughts just moments before? If she knew what was good for her, she would turn around, hop down from the bench and scurry into the ballroom where she could escape from this man and his unwavering gaze.

But she was rooted to the spot, her feet stuck to the bench as though by paste. He was struck by her. By *her*. And he, a duke. It was such a fantastical moment that Evelyn nearly pinched herself to ensure she was not dreaming.

"Your name?" Alverton asked, again.

"I cannot," she replied, her mouth dry. What should he do if he knew at once that she was the poor daughter of a title-less man of little land in a distant county?

Laugh. Surely, this duke would laugh and then retreat.

He continued, "But how might I speak to you if I do not know your name?"

A small smile broke out on her lips. "You are speaking to me now, your grace."

"Will you sing again?" he asked.

Was the man mad? It was one thing to sing quietly to herself. It was entirely different to perform. She shook her head softly and her heart leapt at the apparent disappointment he displayed.

Alverton rocked back on his heels. His eyes flicked to the space behind her and she wondered if he was considering the house she came from.

"You attended Lord Trenton's masquerade," Alverton deduced, "and he is heavily involved in parliament. Do you have a family member in parliament? A husband, perhaps?"

Evelyn shook her head. The duke was clever, indeed, to find such an unobtrusive way to question her marriage status. If that was indeed what he was doing. But how had he known of the masquerade?

Her mask. Of course.

"Then a brother or father?" he asked. "Or perhaps you know Lord Trenton a different way."

"My father, your grace. But he—" She bit her tongue, an idea forming on shaky legs in her mind. She would not tell him of Father's place in the Commons; not yet. With the mask covering her eyes, she was disguised. This was an opportunity which would likely never present itself again.

"Yes?" he asked.

Weighing the brilliance of her plan against possible pitfalls, Evelyn did not allow herself to dwell upon the potential problems. She had never met this man before, and she likely never would again. They did not run in the same social circles, and she was about to leave London, anyway.

And if she had her way, she would not be returning.

"If you must know," she said, glancing back over her shoulder at the ballroom full of people celebrating the close of parliament for the holidays. Lifting her chin, she leveled Alverton with a look. "I am Lady Eve."

Saying the thrilling words aloud sent a chill down her neck and she felt alive, as though announcing her title thus straightened her spine and infused within her a degree of polish. She was no ordinary politician's daughter. She was a *lady*.

Alverton screwed up his eyebrows. "I don't believe we've met before, Lady Eve."

"I reside with my aunt in the country," she explained. She also lived with her father and younger brothers, but those details would only incite more questions.

Adrenaline rushed through her, as if saying the name had transformed her into the woman she claimed to be, and she was filled with courage. "Were you out for a midnight stroll, your grace?"

His mouth turned up in a half-smile. "I was escaping a demanding inquiry."

"Only to force me unwittingly into the same thing?" Her breath caught at the gall of her words, and she seemed to catch Alverton off guard as well. He recovered quickly, however, taking a step closer to the hedge.

"It was not my intent. I merely tired of my own female relations.

They have made it their express resolution to find me a wife. And, you see, I would rather take on the duty alone."

"Have you told them so?"

Alverton paused a moment. "To be honest, I am not sure if I have said so. But I do not hide my irritations."

Evelyn smiled encouragingly. "That is not quite the same thing as communicating your discomfort, your grace. Perhaps they would allow you room to take on the duty alone if you but ask."

"You are singular," he said, his tone curious.

"I must return to my aunt," Evelyn said quickly, afraid she'd gone too far in her advice, "but I thank you for the compliment, your grace."

"Do not leave," he said, taking a swift step closer to the hedge. He seemed to hesitate before saying, "Perhaps I may call on you."

Shaking her head, she said, "I am sorry, your grace. You may not."

Rejection was foreign to this man if his expression was any clue. "And why not?"

"Because that would not be a good idea."

"May I at least have a dance?" he asked.

She glanced to the solid hedge which divided them. Did he intend to jump over it? That was madness.

He pressed his suit. "I was invited to Lord Trenton's masquerade but chose not to attend. It will take me very little time to obtain my mask. If I have been following the music accurately, then I have enough time to arrive before the next set begins." He approached the hedge, reaching forward, his hand just clearing the top.

Evelyn reached over the hedge, allowing Alverton to take her fingers. When his hand closed around her own, her breath caught in her chest. "We might be gone before the next set," she said. Aunt Edith was likely having a spasm of the heart from Evelyn's disappearance. She needed to return to the house forthwith.

His fingers tightened. "Promise me one dance. If nothing else, I should like to have the one dance."

Oh, and how she wished for the same. It could do no harm, surely? He would not know her aunt if he saw her in the ballroom; furthermore, Aunt Edith was regal and haughty enough to ensure that Alverton would not realize the lowness of her birth at first glance.

"Very well," she heard herself say. Belatedly, she added, "Your grace."

His answering grin caused her heart to beat furiously and she snatched her hand back, grabbing onto her skirts in preparation to jump down from the bench.

"I shall see you shortly." Alverton's smooth, masculine timbre floated through the hedge and caused prickles to run down her arms.

She could hear his retreat and took a steadying breath before making her way into the townhouse.

Adjusting the fox mask to be sure it completely covered the majority of her face, she sidled back to Aunt Edith.

"Where have you been?" the old woman snapped, *sotto voce*.

"I needed a breath of fresh air."

Aunt Edith glanced over her shoulder, sending Evelyn a wrinkled glare. It had been reckless and foolish. But if Aunt Edith was aware that Evelyn had met a duke and he was en route to dance with her, the old woman would not be complaining. She was an incurable title-hunter.

"Do not disappear again if you want to retain any semblance of a reputation."

It was on the edge of Evelyn's tongue to explain that she had been alone in the garden, but that was not entirely true, so she kept quiet.

Waiting for the music to end and the door to open was like watching sap drip from a tree: painfully slow.

When the door finally opened and the white-wigged servant in red livery announced *his* name, Evelyn turned at once. Alverton was as tall as he had appeared in the dim moonlight of the garden. A black half-mask tied around his head resembled a wolf. His hair was dark, tousled as though he'd brushed it aside with his fingers and let it be. His face was shaded with a few days' whiskers—adding to the rugged nature of his wolf costume. When his eyes flicked about as he searched the group for her, her breath stalled.

One by one the people on the outskirts of the ballroom seemed to notice the duke. Evelyn's heart rate increased each time he paused in conversation. Had she made a horrible mistake in accepting? She was about to draw undue attention to herself.

The moment Alverton's eyes came to rest on her, she decided that she had not erred so greatly. Not when he was at the ball for her. He crossed the room with long, purposeful strides, coming to stop just before Aunt Edith.

"Your grace," Evelyn cut in quickly. "Allow me to present my aunt, Mrs. Chadwick."

Aunt Edith appeared as though she'd swallowed a frog.

But Alverton did little more than bow to her before turning his attention fully on Evelyn. The music had paused along with the duke's entrance and a moment later people began to line up for another dance. He watched her closely before offering his arm.

Quirking up his lips in a devastatingly handsome half-smile, he said, "I believe this is my dance."

CHAPTER 2

*L*ady Eve danced as well as she sang. Alverton watched her flow smoothly through the transitions. He would have chosen a less lively country dance, had he known, but it was better than nothing. Though graceful, she seemed skittish, like an unbroken horse, and he wanted to be careful.

This was the first woman to intrigue him in years. He'd seen nothing of her face besides the striking green of her eyes and the shape of her chin, but he was drawn to her. And after the slew of matchmaking mamas—his own included—and unrelenting flirts, Lady Eve's reluctance was refreshing. Had he really told her he wished to call on her? It was forward of him and would have pleased his mother and grandmother to no end.

He, the Duke of Alverton, had done his very best to avoid title-greedy women for the better part of a year. But he could only do so much and his mother was constantly throwing women into his path.

Was he mad? He did not wish to truly pursue Lady Eve—he'd only wanted to hear her sing again. And yet, his request to call had been summarily rejected.

After she'd been told of his title.

That was not something which had ever before happened to

Alverton and he'd been momentarily stunned. If he did not know better, he would assume she had placed him under a spell with her low, velvety voice. He was usually such a calm, rational creature, but the sound of Lady Eve softly singing had done something to his soul.

They separated in the movement of the dance and he watched her as she glided back toward him. The mask adorning her face was a work of art, but he could clearly see her eyes underneath it and he believed them to be just as lovely as the jewels which surrounded them. The amber on the mask was just the right color and highlighted her green eyes, making them all the brighter.

Or, perhaps that was due to the exertion of dancing.

Alverton had been utterly chilled earlier when they met outside, but the heat of the ballroom forced him to wish he was in the garden once again. Perhaps after the dance he would forgo a conversation with her aunt and beg Lady Eve's company for a turn about the garden.

No, that was madness. There was a reason the doors were closed and they had been the only people outside earlier. It was frigid. He'd only gone to the garden himself to escape the women in his house.

Lady Eve returned to his side and he took her hands as part of the dance. The gloves which separated them were soft and smooth, and Alverton imagined her skin was much the same.

But why didn't he know her? He had thought he knew every man or woman with a title in London, but evidently, he was mistaken. He examined her hair, the chestnut brown a simple color, which could easily belong to a host of women.

Her carriage was straight and elegant, her movements graceful. She certainly had the bearings of a lady, but otherwise he was lost as to who she could be.

The song came to a close and Alverton found himself opposite Lady Eve once again, bowing to her. A man called out the quadrille and they moved into place for the next dance.

"Have you lived in London all your life?" he asked.

She glanced up at him, her chest rising and falling rapidly as she caught her breath from the previous dance. Her intelligent eyes searched his. "No. I have come for this Season alone."

A vague answer, of course. "For parliament?"

Lady Eve nodded, looking back to where her aunt sat watching them with an eagle eye. He felt the older woman's gaze prickle his flesh and knew immediately that *she* was a matchmaking woman of the worst sort.

He would do his best to stay away from Lady Eve's aunt, he vowed.

"Yet you are here now, Lady Eve. And you don't wish for me to call on you."

Lady Eve glanced about them as though wondering who could overhear. It was all he could do not to laugh at her nervousness. Why did she worry about who might overhear? They were in costume, after all.

"I am not planning to return to London, your grace. And we leave in the morning to travel home. It is simply illogical, that is all. I meant no offense."

Alverton gazed at her as the motions of the dance continued. Why was she so sensible? Women of his acquaintance certainly weren't. Each new revelation about her character intrigued him further.

Perhaps it would not be madness after all if he was to find a way to call on her. Getting to know her better certainly wouldn't be a horrible idea. And surely it would please the women in his life.

But, if she was leaving London, then she was correct. It did not seem feasible.

They danced together for the duration of the music and all the while Alverton watched Lady Eve, examining her graceful movements. He searched his mind for a way to see her again, but by the time the final strains of the quadrille drew to an end, he was no closer to contriving a way to make it work.

Alverton was not the sort of man to give up easily, but even he could see that Lady Eve was correct. Unless…

"Which county do you reside in? And what is the name of your estate?" he asked her as she was straightening from her curtsy.

Her eyes widened. Had that been too forward of him?

"Your grace, are you in your cups?"

A loud, booming laugh wrenched from his gut and traveled out of his mouth. He'd caught her off guard with his mirth, but her question had shocked him. What sort of woman asked a duke if he was drunk? It was a valid question, he supposed, given his erratic behavior, but shocking all the same.

"No, my lady. I am utterly sensible this evening."

Her eyebrows were covered by the mask she wore, but Alverton imagined her brow being raised by the slight widening of one eye. *Touché, mademoiselle*. Perhaps sensible was a bit of a stretch.

He felt as though his head was spinning. Offering her his arm, he led Lady Eve back to her aunt. He opened his mouth to speak but was cut off once again.

"Father wished us home long before now, Aunt. Perhaps we ought to leave."

The older woman glared at her niece before turning back to the duke and waiting for him to speak.

"I thank you for allowing me the privilege of dancing with your niece, madam," he said.

"Of course, your grace," Mrs. Chadwick replied. Her beady, hungry eyes raked him over and the hair on the back of his neck stood on end.

He turned to Lady Eve, lifting her hand in his own. "Thank you for the pleasure."

Eyes began to warm his back and a quick glance around the surrounding area informed him that if he were to stay a moment longer, he would be required to beg more dances from the young ladies in attendance.

Which was something he heartily wished to avoid. It was the very reason he had chosen *not* to attend this masquerade in the first place.

Offering Lady Eve and her aunt a bow, Alverton said, "I must bid you goodnight."

He drank in one last look at Lady Eve before turning on his heel and exiting the room in swift, purposeful strides.

Alverton nodded to his host on his way out, his mask covering only half his face and not sufficient to guard his identity. A brisk walk around the block to his own house was all he needed to clear his head, however. And one thing was abundantly clear to him: Lady Eve was unlike any woman he had met before.

※

THE DUCHESS, Alverton's mother, was every bit as regal as a queen. She sat upon her throne-like chair at the breakfast table, watching her son through narrowed eyes. "Henny tells me you went out last night," she finally said.

Ah. So she had deduced his social activity with help from the butler. Alverton yawned, his sleep having been horribly broken with unfinished feelings and memories of Lady Eve. The mystery of who she was plagued him above all else and he regretted not pressing her further for information. Taking a bite of his toasted bread, he chewed slowly to draw out the moment longer.

She continued, "And evidently, you had a mask on."

Drat Henny. The butler was not very loyal, was he? No, that was unfair. Clearly he was loyal to the duchess.

She picked up her cup of tea, sipping the liquid slowly while watching her son over the rim of her cup. For all of her years, the duchess had retained the majority of her beauty, small hairline wrinkles about her eyes and mouth the only signs of age.

"You attended a masquerade?"

"It was a small affair," Alverton answered quickly, flicking his hand in dismissal. "I made a short appearance."

But it was far more than he'd done in recent months intentionally, and certainly more than he'd ever done without the express persuasion of his mother and grandmother.

"Is there a particular *reason* you chose to attend?" she asked.

He would give up his left hand in order to honestly say that he had *not* attended for a particular woman, but that would be lying. And Alverton did not lie.

"I must go," he said, standing. "Sanders is expecting me."

Disappointment fell over his mother's features and Alverton's gut wrenched. It was a familiar expression. He'd seen it more than anything else over the course of the previous year. But it could not be helped. Mother wished for him to marry above all else; and he did not.

He paused at the door and looked back. It was on the tip of his tongue to ask if she knew a Lady Eve, or any lords connected to a Mrs. Chadwick, but he did not wish to show his cards just yet. "Good day, Mother," he said, offering her a smile. "Give Grandmother a kiss for me."

She merely grunted, unamused. And he left.

Sanders was half-awake when Alverton located the gentleman within the man's own drawing room. The earl's shirt hung open, his waistcoat untied.

"It's early to call, Alverton," Sanders said, stifling a yawn as his pale blue eyes attempted to focus on his friend. Alverton dropped onto the sofa opposite him. Sanders' eyes narrowed. "And yet, you look wide awake."

"I am finished with London," Alverton said with dramatic flair.

"Because..." Sanders prompted, leaning back comfortably.

Alverton cast his gaze to the ceiling, huffing in irritation. "The same frustrations I've complained of since my father's mourning period was over."

Sanders nodded knowingly. "Women." He paused. "Or, your mother?"

"Both."

"What is it this time?" Sanders asked.

Alverton scrubbed a hand over his face. "I am bound to sound mad."

Sanders merely settled into his sofa cushion further, leaning his head back in both hands as if to say, *I have all day.*

"I met a lady last night," Alverton explained, "but she is not interested in allowing me to call on her. She refused to give me her direction, if you can credit it."

Sanders chuckled. "How odd."

"You mock me, but I have never before been rejected. It is foreign to me."

Sitting up in his seat, Sanders asked, "Are you bothered by the rejection, or the woman who delivered it?"

"Both. But she has left London and does not intend to return. Meanwhile, I cannot seem to escape the hordes of mothers who wish to tie their daughters to my title." He shivered, recalling the hungry eyes that watched him during the masquerade.

"Perhaps I ought to be grateful I am only an earl," Sanders said, his face carefully void of expression. "It must be horrid to be so sought after."

"You joke, Sanders. But it is indeed a trial."

His friend's face searched his own, and Alverton had the impression that the earl truly *did* realize the extent of his burden. They'd been friends since they were boys together at school, and nobody in England knew Alverton as well as Sanders did. Sanders saw firsthand how Alverton could not go anywhere without being inundated with debutantes and their greedy mothers.

His own father, the eighth Duke of Alverton, had been a man of the best sort and Alverton wished to follow in his footsteps. Yet, following his father's code as a gentleman had forced Alverton to offer far too many dances of courtesy or rides in the park to simpering ladies. He did his best to be pleasing when he left his house, but it was tiring.

And he was very, very tired.

"You look exhausted," Sanders said, his voice growing deep and serious. "Perhaps you were right. You ought to take a break from Society."

Alverton nodded in agreement. He'd considered this matter himself over recent months, however, and was convinced the only way he could truly get the break he needed was by marrying one of the obnoxious twits who vied for his title. And he simply could not stomach that.

Sanders looked him in the eye. "I am traveling to my mother's country house in Wiltshire until parliament resumes. You are welcome to join me if you wish. We don't go there often, but it's a good place for a respite."

Alverton paused, catching Sanders' eye. "Do you mean it?"

"Of course," he answered at once. "My mother and sisters left weeks ago for my aunt's house in Cheshire, so I am afraid it would only be the two of us."

"All the better," Alverton muttered. This was precisely what he needed. To get away to a house in the countryside where he could breathe once again. A place he could venture outside without fear of being set upon by a slew of women.

"I do not have grand plans for Christmas or Twelfth Night, I am afraid, but we can celebrate quietly. Do you think your mother will mind terribly if you leave?"

"She has Grandmother to keep her company," Alverton said, feeling the balm of a break from his family already. He turned to his friend. "When do we go?"

CHAPTER 3

The house smelled precisely as it had when they left it a few months prior. The only missing thing Evelyn found once she stepped within its doors was the sound of two rambunctious nine-year-olds running about the corridors and yelling things like *you will never get away from me!* and *stop right there before I tie you up and feed you to the pigs!*

"I am fatigued," Aunt Edith said, dragging herself toward the stairs. "Do not bother me for dinner this evening. I shall have a tray in my room."

Evelyn watched her aunt retreat. The woman sounded as though she sat on death's doorstep, but the reality was quite the opposite. She was not a weak woman, though she affected such a persona. And the evidence was in her constant vigilance in chaperoning Evelyn about London. Even when Evelyn dozed after one of their countless late nights during the Season, Aunt Edith was forever on her guard.

Evelyn faced the butler standing post beside the front door. "Where are the boys?" she inquired.

"In the grove, Miss Trainor."

She should have known. Turning to her father, she said, "I will go fetch them."

"But the cold," he argued, his mustache quivering in concern. He wobbled on his cane and Evelyn stepped forward at once. The boys could wait.

"Come, father. Let's get you settled in the library."

Evelyn strung an arm around her father's back and helped him as his cane supported him down the corridor. They stepped into the library, a long room lined with bookcases, and toward the soft leather chairs set over a blue rug before the fireplace.

After helping him into the chair, Evelyn moved to the fire and used the poker to bring it back to life.

"You should not do that," Father said. "Fetch a servant."

Evelyn couldn't help but smile. "How silly to fetch a servant when it will take me just a moment to do it myself." She straightened, wiping her hands against the skirt of her chocolate brown gown. *This* was why she wore serviceable, purposeful dresses. The dirt seemed to blend in better.

"Did you enjoy the masquerade? I've yet to ask you about it," her father said as Evelyn took a chair on the other side of the carpet, tucking her feet under her. The large chair dwarfed her, but she found it comfortable. It was home, after all.

"It was amusing," she said at last.

Father's knowing gaze watched her. "In what sense?"

She could not tell him about meeting the duke in the garden. But surely Aunt Edith had already informed him of the dance.

"I danced with a duke," she said with little flair. "He was very tall."

Father brought his hand up and scratched his chin. "I cannot deduce if that is a point in his favor or against it."

"Neither," Evelyn answered, doing her utmost to sound unaffected. "He mistook me for a proper lady, Father. We shall never speak again, so it is of little consequence."

The explanation was both honest and a simple way to explain Alverton's *odd behavior* in requesting her dance. Evelyn had searched her brain to find a way to explain to her family why Alverton had crossed the floor with direct purpose to dance with her, and she had determined that the truth was the only way to go. He *had* mistaken her for a lady. Of course, it was due to her own initial misleading, but that was neither here nor there.

The point remained that the Duke of Alverton would never request *Evelyn's* hand for a dance. He only had eyes for Lady Eve.

And regardless, she was going to do her best to convince her father not to return to London after Twelfth Night.

She regarded him carefully as his eyelids drifted closed. His skin was pale and wrinkled, and she believed more lines had developed on his face during the short drive from London. Why could he not accept that it was better for his health if he stepped down from his political seat? His sons would benefit from his presence at home and his daughter would be satisfied if she never left Wiltshire again. Could she persuade him? It was certainly worth a shot.

Standing, she crossed to the chest on the far side of the room and lifted the throw lying on top of it. Her mother had knitted the blanket and Evelyn often found comfort in its warm embrace. She brought it to her nose, inhaling. It no longer smelled of her mother, but it did smell of the house.

Evelyn laid it over her slumbering father and stole one last look at his peaceful face before taking her leave of the room. She must find a way to convince him to remain in Wiltshire. And she had just a fortnight to do so.

❄

FINDING her brothers had been easy.

After obtaining her cape and tying the ribbons about her neck, Evelyn took off toward the forest and the large, thick oak tree nestled snugly within the grove of trees. Sanders Grove had been vainly named for the peerage who owned the land, but the earl's family wasn't in residence very often. Evelyn and her brothers had grown up playing within the trees and never came to any trouble from it. Her father's property stopped just before the tree line, but the Earl of Sanders had never before complained of small footprints in the mud or the odd game of militia between her brothers and neighboring tenant children when he was in residence.

The grove had grown thinner with its loss of leaves. Cold seeped up from the frozen ground and into Evelyn's boots. She found the familiar deer path and followed its winding, unclear way through the trees toward the place she would likely find her brothers.

She was not ten paces away when she finally heard low voices discussing something of great importance just above her own height.

She had been correct. They were in the tree.

Evelyn approached the old, massive tree quietly, calling on her own experience playing with neighboring children and the lightness of foot required in an important snowball match. She made it to the base of the thick, squat tree without being detected, and circled it slowly until she found a good root to climb upon.

The tree was hundreds, if not thousands of years old, and the thick trunk showed it. It was as wide as Evelyn was tall, which created a large, flat area from which its branches stretched out. The tree was perfect for childhood games. Large, long limbs branched out in multiple directions as though the tree itself was doing its best to reach the four corners of the grove.

Finding purchase on a taller root, Evelyn counted silently to five before jumping into view of the main, flat center of the tree and shouting, "Found you!"

Two young faces covered in freckles and topped with fiery red hair turned to her in sudden surprise, their features a mixture of shock and fright.

"Evelyn!" Jack yelled. She could not tell if he was excited or angry until he ran across the tree and jumped down, coming around to hug her about the ankles.

"Evelyn!" Harry echoed, doing very much the same thing while remaining in the tree, his grimy arms slithering around her neck.

"Boys," Evelyn said, her voice muffled by Harry's arms. "Allow me to climb down and then I can hug you properly."

They reluctantly let go and she hopped down from the root just before her younger brothers nearly bowled her over again.

"Harry! Jack! You must allow me to breathe," Evelyn said through peals of laughter. "I have missed you, too."

Jack stepped back first, eyeing her. "Are you married now?"

"What? Why ever would you say such a thing?" she asked, laughing.

Jack did not laugh, however. His young, serious eyes watched her closely. "Because I heard Father telling Aunt Edith that you would not return home until you found a husband."

She grew still. Well, that certainly explained why Aunt Edith had forced her to attend the masquerade the evening before they left London. And the other balls, dinners, and card parties Aunt Edith had feigned interest in. They had been working together to find Evelyn a husband.

And yet, they hadn't met with success. Was that why Father had appeared so downtrodden and sullen during the carriage ride home from London? Evelyn had chalked it up to his feeling poorly, but Jack's new information caused her to reevaluate.

"*We* are glad you aren't getting married," Harry said. "Now you can be our damsel."

"I'm not sure I'm feeling up to being a damsel today," Evelyn said, her shoulders deflating. It was difficult not to feel like a failure now that she knew of Father's plans. Sure, she had realized Aunt Edith was hoping she would marry—the woman had very obviously pushed her to attend social functions. But she hadn't been aware of how deeply *Father* was hoping to be rid of her.

"Tomorrow?" the boys asked in unison, their large, green eyes imploring her in a way they knew would get them precisely what they asked for.

Evelyn could not help but smile. "Yes, tomorrow. But for now, let us return to the house. The sun will be going down soon, and I very much wish for you to tell me what you've been up to while we've been away."

❄

THE FOLLOWING morning Evelyn made it outside before the sun. She'd awoken early, unable to shake the knowledge that she was a burden on her father. She had thought she was *helpful*; that she was lightening his load and giving him more time to heal from whatever it was that ailed him. He'd seen doctors, or so he claimed, but he refused to inform her what they'd told him.

Evelyn huffed, her breath clouding before her on the winding path through the woods. She was going to call on Julia far too early, but she had a feeling it would be forgiven.

The sun rose during her walk through the trees and by the time Evelyn left the other side of the grove, the sun had peaked above Lord Sanders' enormous manor house in the distance and warmed her skin. She followed the road until it forked and took the left lane toward Derham, away from the earl's property. It was farther away than she had recalled, and by the time she reached Julia's house it was no longer an inappropriate hour to pay a call.

Nestled among a row of tightly-huddled, tall houses, the Cooper house was set apart from the rest by its freshly painted door and polished brass knocker.

Bringing her fist up to tap on the solid, wooden door, Evelyn stepped back and surveyed the front of the house. Made of stone and covered in a thick blanket of ivy vines, Julia lived in a house sandwiched among a row of buildings. A female servant came to the door and admitted Evelyn at once, ushering her into the warm parlor before bustling back out.

"Evelyn, you are home!" Julia's familiar voice was a balm on Evelyn's frosted exterior and she deemed the cold walk worth it once her vision fell upon her friend. In a light gray muslin dress, her blonde hair pulled back in a simple knot, Julia looked lovely and familiar. "You must tell me all about London."

"Indeed," Evelyn said, "I shall. But it is good to be home."

The old friends settled onto the sofa after Julia called for tea and chatted much like they had their entire lives—quickly and with purpose. Julia filled Evelyn in on the happenings around Derham during her absence, and Evelyn described the balls and masquerades she had attended in Town.

"But you mean to tell me you found *no* man worth pursuing?" Julia asked, doubtful. The delicate planes of her face screwed up, causing small lines to form between her eyebrows and on her nose. "I have a hard time believing all London men to be toads and pigs."

Evelyn shook her head. Her traitorous mind recalled Alverton stepping into the ballroom, tall and handsome, during the masquerade and how thoroughly Evelyn's heart had flipped over, but that was ridiculous. He was out of reach, and not worth mentioning.

Julia, however, knew her friend quite well. "What are you thinking of? A stallion among the swine?"

A moment's hesitation was enough to give Evelyn away and Julia continued, primly folding her hands in her lap. "You must tell me now for I know you have a secret and I shall not rest until I am apprised of it."

Evelyn glanced to the open door.

Julia followed her gaze but shook her head, bringing a lock of pale hair loose. "My brother was gone all evening on a call and will not be awake yet. The Taylor's youngest child was given to fever a few days ago and then the mother took ill. It swept through all six children after that and last night, I believe, was the worst of it."

"How horrible," Evelyn said, bringing her hand up to cover her heart. "They are fortunate to have your brother so near. Are they in need of anything?"

"I am sure they would appreciate a hot meal, but Jared told the maids this morning that Mrs. Taylor's fever had broken before he left their house and he expects the children to recover."

"We can only pray," Evelyn said.

Julia nodded. "Now, you cannot expect me to have forgotten so easily. Do tell."

Evelyn leaned forward on the sofa, lowering her voice. "Do you recall Lady Eve?"

"The game we played as children?"

"Yes, of sorts." Julia had always been simply Lady Julia—she lacked Evelyn's imagination—when, as children, they had pretended to be ladies of quality. But they had not participated in the game in many years. That is, they had not played it *together*. Evelyn still did her fair share of daydreaming in secret.

Evelyn continued, telling Julia of the shocking discovery of the duke in the garden. "I would not have sung had I known that a duke stood on the other side of the hedge. And though he could see me, the shadows and the dark made it impossible for me to see him until I stood on the bench and looked over the hedge."

Julia chuckled, pulling a loose lock of blonde hair and tucking it back into her knot. "I hope you delivered a curtsy worthy of such a performance."

"I did not even consider it."

"A missed opportunity," Julia said. Her eyes widened, her pale brows rising. "You must go on. What did the duke say?"

"He asked to call on me and I refused."

Julia scoffed.

"I did agree to a dance, however," Evelyn said, unable to restrain her smile. "And it was glorious. He was dashing, dressed as a wolf. And I felt like I was dancing on clouds in his arms."

"When shall you see him again?" Julia asked, her head tilted in compassion.

Evelyn swallowed, lowering her gaze. "I cannot. I stood on that bench in the back garden and found a chance to pretend I was *truly* Lady Eve, and I introduced myself as such. He believes me to be a lady, Julia. He would never have pursued me otherwise, so I must put him from my mind and take care to remain unaffected by his memory." Evelyn leaned back and searched her friend's face.

Julia's voice was hesitant, her eyebrows drawn down. "But what shall you do if you see him again?"

"I won't," Evelyn said easily. "I never have before. And I am planning to remain here. I won't be returning to London."

Julia's pale eyebrows rose. "Your father has given his blessing? Or has he chosen to retire?"

"Not yet, but I have made it my objective to convince him. I am not sure he will last another parliamentary session, Julia."

Her friend reached forward and lifted Evelyn's hand, squeezing it. "Let me know how I may help."

"Of course." Evelyn rose. "I must be off. Oh, how I've missed you."

She made her way to the front door, glancing over her shoulder when she thought she heard a creak on the stairs behind her, but no one was there. Bidding Julia a final goodbye, Evelyn stepped onto the cobblestone street toward home.

A carriage rumbled down the street behind her and she flattened herself against the brick building to give the horses room to pass. The crest emblazoned on the side of the carriage in green and yellow indicated that the Earl of Sanders—or one of his sisters, perhaps—rode inside. Evelyn watched them ramble past her and stepped into the road after they had cleared.

She would need to inform her brothers so they might be mindful of their games within the grove. But if history was any indication, whoever came to Chesford Place wouldn't likely remain long.

The drape covering the back window of the carriage moved aside and a face appeared in the small square, catching her eye. She paused on the road, tilting her head in confusion at the familiarity of the eyes behind the glass.

It was not until the carriage turned down the road and disappeared from sight that she realized at once whom those striking eyes belonged to. They were the eyes of her duke.

CHAPTER 4

Alverton looked through the back window of the carriage as they rolled down the cobblestone street and then around a bend. The woman who stood against the brick wall had looked so familiar to him that he watched her as long as he could. But alas, he could not place where he recognized her from.

"We shall be forced to dine with the Hollingsfords, I'm afraid, once they hear that we're in residence," Sanders said without missing a beat. Evidently, he hadn't been arrested by the sight of a woman standing on the side of the road as Alverton had. "They are an unavoidable acquaintance. But Hollingsford is a tolerable gentleman and puts up a decent game and sufficient drink to make the dinner party worth attending."

"You make Derham Society sound like quite a treat," Alverton grumbled.

Sanders' smile was wide and unforgiving, his blue eyes sparkling. "We don't come here often. And there isn't much here in the way of gentry, but there's enough to keep us company when we tire of ourselves."

Alverton's mind wandered to the woman in the road. What was it about her eyes that entreated him so?

"You seem distracted," Sanders said, jostling along with the carriage on the bumpy lane.

Alverton shook his head as though the action itself would lift his confusion. "The woman we passed in the street earlier looked familiar, but I cannot place where I've seen her before."

"Can't say that I saw her," Sanders replied, lifting a shoulder. He was of no help at all. "You'll recall the woods I told you of? We'll find some fine sport there."

"I recall the hedge you could not jump," Alverton responded, amusement coloring his tone. "I should like to see it with my own eyes."

Sanders shot his friend a rueful smile before turning to watch out the window. "I told you of that when I was soundly foxed. I hadn't intended for it to be remembered."

The carriage pulled from the main road and down a rocky lane lined with trees. They bounced along, jostling softly as the wheels rolled on packed, hard ground. A large building of dark stone rose into sight and Alverton grinned at the gothic house.

"This is the perfect setting for my escape from the *ton*."

"You did tell your mother where you would be, I assume," Sanders said, though the concern in his voice proved his disbelief.

Alverton watched the large, imposing building grow as they approached. "Yes. She knows I've come to your house, I merely forgot to specify *which* house of yours we escaped to. But what choice did I have? She was quite displeased when I told her. Just prior to my announcement, she explained to me that we were going to be entertaining her sister's children for a fortnight. Do you remember what my cousin did the last time they came to London?"

Sanders stared at him. "Remind me."

"The oldest cousin—Miss Cassandra Rowe is her name—begged me to teach her the art of billiards. When I finally relented, she did her best to compromise me. In my own house." Alverton watched his friend struggle to remain composed. "It is not humorous, you know. It is downright nonsensical."

The carriage rolled to a stop and Sanders hopped out onto the gravel drive. Alverton followed him, stretching his back as snow began to fall. "It isn't nonsensical," Sanders argued, beginning toward the house. "It is rather brilliant if the girl wishes to become a duchess."

It was a blessed thing Alverton knew his friend so well, for he could tell at once the man was being facetious. He ignored the comment, climbing the shallow front steps to the house and following Sanders into the open doorway. The bitter cold followed them into the foyer, swirling about them as small snowflakes melted on their shoulders and clung stubbornly to the ends of their hair.

The servants followed them inside bearing their trunks and Sanders instructed the housekeeper to direct Alverton to his room.

With deference, the stout woman led Alverton up a curved staircase and to a chamber located farther down the corridor. She curtsied her way from the room and beat a hasty escape once Alverton stepped inside. He spun a slow circle, appreciating the simplicity of the furniture and large windows which lined the opposite wall. Crossing to the window, Alverton peeled back the heavy, green drapes, sweeping his gaze over the thick woods which were slowly becoming frosted by snow.

He could not remove from his mind the woman they had passed on the road earlier. Her face swam before him as though she was a ghost reflecting in the windowpanes and he narrowed his gaze, concentrating on the woman's features and trying to determine how he knew her.

He'd only been a duke for the last two years, but he'd been served and bowed to, adored and flattered by many people in that time, as a man with immense fortune and power should be. He'd been around countless women over the years, but never before had he been so struck by a woman's face. Her beauty was simple, but regal.

And it killed him that he could not place her.

Perhaps she was a servant of some sort and he simply could not recall where she'd assisted him—but her clothes and bearing proclaimed otherwise. Besides, he had never been one to toy with servants, and hardly looked at them for longer than a breath.

That must be it. The only reason he could not place her now was because he must have last seen her in a different location. It was the *place* which threw him, and not the girl. She could have passed by him in a local inn wherein he had previously stopped to feed his horses and himself. He'd traveled through Wiltshire just a few months prior on his way to Bristol. He must have seen her there.

Contented by his judgment, he stepped back from the window, allowing the drapes to swing closed.

※

THIS WAS no direct cause for panic. Or so Evelyn told herself.

Surely the duke was simply passing through—or perhaps it was a trick of the light. The sun had been shining against the small carriage window and Evelyn had, admittedly, thought of Alverton quite frequently since the masquerade.

It was not such a stretch of the imagination to assume she had not truly seen the duke, but simply *imagined* she saw the duke.

Yes, that must be it.

Closing the front door behind her, Evelyn shed her cape and bonnet and dropped them into the butler's outstretched arms. Letting herself into the library, she found her father in his favorite leather chair, his head resting against the back of the high, wingback cushion.

His pale face aged each consecutive parliament session. How could he not see that it was bad for his health?

"I can sense you watching me," Father said, surprising her.

"Forgive me. I did not intend to intrude on your nap."

His eyes opened, an amused smile crossing his mouth. "I was not sleeping, Evelyn. I was merely thinking with my eyes closed."

"No one would think ill of you if you were."

Her father sat up straighter, piercing her with a look. "I am not an elderly man and I am perfectly capable of remaining awake as long as I please. You needn't treat me like a child, Evelyn. That is my duty as your parent, and not the reverse."

Evelyn's cheeks warmed. "You must realize that I care. I do not set out to be bothersome."

They stood upon a thin, invisible bridge, both pulling the other across it in the direction they thought best. Evelyn had the upper hand, however, for she *knew* her way to be the better course of action. What she was lacking was the ability to convince him, evidently.

His eyes softened. "Then cease, my dear. I promise you I can care for myself."

"Will you not agree to see Dr. Cooper? If only you would allow him to simply—"

"Evelyn," Father said harshly, the amused light gone from his eyes. "Enough."

Her heart raced as she got to her feet. "Yes, Father," she said. "I will leave you now."

She turned to go, hoping he would request she remain. But he did not. Hurt sliced through her at the dismissal, but she had brought it upon herself with her excessive pressing. Blowing a stray lock of hair up and away from her face, Evelyn climbed the stairs toward her own bedchamber.

"Evelyn," a brittle voice called from the foyer.

She glanced over her shoulder, her gaze coming to rest on Aunt Edith standing in the parlor doorway.

"Yes?"

"If you would be so kind as to fetch my shawl I would be indebted to you. It is positively frigid in this room."

Swallowing her annoyance, Evelyn nodded. "Of course."

She turned back up the stairs, her hand trailing the bannister as her jaw clenched repeatedly. Father never wanted her help, but Aunt Edith required too much of it at times. She did not mind fetching a shawl here or there, but she was not a personal servant. They paid others for that duty.

Letting herself into Aunt Edith's room, she picked up the yellow shawl from the edge of the bed and ran her hands over the soft material. Things needed to change, and she was going to be the one to make that happen.

CHAPTER 5

Sanders was a terrific host. He provided good food, good drink, and plenty of time to oneself. Alverton sat at the table long after Sanders drifted to sleep, his friend's head lolling onto his shoulder and his empty glass resting loosely in his hand upon the table. Alverton picked up his own glass and drained the remaining liquid before setting it softly on the table.

Was it foolish to run from Town? From his mother? She was relentless in her search for the next duchess, but her heart was in a good place. Or so he assumed. Her thinly veiled comments about securing the line and giving her an heir and a spare prior to her death were effective in pushing him further from her ultimate goal.

He was aware of his duties and the responsibility he held, but at only eight-and-twenty, he was still young. He had plenty of time. And the women his mother deemed worthy were nothing worthy of note.

No, the few women who made it past Mother and Grandmother's rigid guidelines were all very much the same. They either came from old, distinguished families of money and title, with meekness to rival a sofa cushion and the wit of a four-year-old, or they were entirely inappropriate.

But little did Mother know, the women she was parading for his pleasure were not the perfect specimens she believed them to be. Lady Hester, who had been introduced to Alverton at a recent ball, had snuck off after supper with Mr. Halpert, unbeknownst to anyone but Alverton and his fortunate wandering gaze.

Then he'd been forced to partner Miss Rupert, the wealthy niece of an earl, in whist for an evening and she proved she had naught but pudding for brains. And the woman he'd been coerced to take into dinner the night before the masquerade had been so frightened of him that she had stared at her plate the entire evening and had not consumed a single bite.

But Lady Eve defied it all. She had not gone to the garden to meet a beau; she had gone to be alone. Of that he was almost certain, and her solemn singing had only proved his assumption further. He'd been unable to see anything of her face beyond her eyes and the cut of her jaw, as her mask covered most of her face. But Alverton was certain she was guileless—an admirable trait when he'd spent his life being bowed and scraped to by people with impure motivations.

And besides that, she was a *lady*. Lady Eve was worthy of becoming the next duchess, whatever her background.

A clock chimed in the hallway, startling Alverton from his shocking line of thought and causing Sanders to stir beside him. He would be ashamed of his rash jump from a woman he shared a dance with, to someone he considered worthy of courting, but he could not deny the feeling he'd had when he was speaking to her.

She was honest and good. Of that, he was absolutely certain. If there was any trait he found necessary in a future wife, it was honesty. His own father had taught him the importance of dealing truthfully with others and he found immense value in it.

He knew he sounded mad in his mind, but he could not help his thoughts. He needed to find this woman. He could question his acquaintances when he returned to Town. *Someone* would know her, surely.

"How late is the hour?" a groggy Sanders inquired, his hands coming up to rub his eyes.

"Too late," Alverton answered. "I was about to wake you. Say, have you any information about a woman by the name of Lady Eve?"

Sanders shook his head, his sleepy eyes half-closed.

"Or a Mrs. Chadwick?"

"Doesn't ring a bell. Sorry, chap."

He should have known it wouldn't be so easy. He and Sanders ran in the same crowds, anyway. Sighing, he pushed up from the table. Patience and restraint did not come naturally to him, but they were skills he'd honed over the last decade of dealing with his mother and grandmother.

And apparently, he was going to perfect them further.

※

Alverton arose early and breakfasted efficiently before fetching a stallion from the stables. The cold air whipped around his head as he took off for the grove lining Sanders' property, the cold prickling his nostrils. Snow had covered the ground during the night and he glanced over his shoulder to find hoof prints over the powdery ground.

The holiday was bound to be a blessed retreat. He was grateful for his mother's guidance, of course, and Grandmother's stern opinions had taught him just the right way to hold himself in public, but being away from them was always a bit of a relief.

Leading the horse onto a game trail through the woods, Alverton was overtaken at once by the mystical feeling within the trees. The snow had created a sort of sound barrier and when combined with the wall of trees, the farther he trailed into the wood, the more he felt utterly alone.

And he loved it. It was an escape on another level.

A soft, subdued humming met his ears and he turned his head to listen for the sound. It was familiar in a way that set his heart beating rapidly.

Directing the horse toward the right, he followed the humming as it turned into tranquil singing. Alverton's heart began to gallop as he approached a small open space with a large, thick tree in the center of the clearing. He knew this voice. The tone and the tune were both very familiar and he could not believe his own luck.

The song grew clearer as he pulled back on the reins and squeezed his knees softly into the horse's sides. Coming to a complete halt, Alverton quietly slid from the saddle, guiding the horse to a nearby tree and tying the reins securely to a low branch.

He rested his hand on the side of the horse's neck and listened, his body humming with anticipation. Could it be? It *sounded* like Lady Eve's rich, alto voice had been transported to this very grove. But that would be crazy, would it not?

Alverton's hand slipped from the horse's neck as he took a step toward the gargantuan tree. If he had created the singing of his own imagination, then he would know of his own madness and push her from his mind at once. But if not? Well, there was only one way to find out.

※

COLD SEEPED through the cape Evelyn wore and began to chill her skin. She pulled her legs close and dropped her forehead onto her knees. She'd come out to the massive tree in Sanders Grove to look for her brothers but neither of them had been here. Instead, she'd sat on the flat base in the center of the imposing tree and listened to the quiet calmness of the wood after a fresh snowfall.

Father was going to be the death of Evelyn, she just knew it. If he refused to see Julia's brother, Jared Cooper, of his own accord, then Evelyn was going to drag Dr. Cooper to her house and force the men to come to an arrangement. She'd coerce and blackmail, if need be. Dr. Cooper had been a few years older than she and Julia, but he'd agreed to play with them on occasion as children and she was sure she could dig up a distressing anecdote to share with the town if he did not comply.

It was not kind, perhaps, but it would no doubt be effective. She had no intention of *actually* sharing an anecdote; she would only use the threat as a way to force Dr. Cooper to help.

Humming, she recalled the earlier years of her life, when her mother had come to her room each and every evening to sing her to sleep. She'd had the voice of an angel and Evelyn often imagined herself standing before a crowd of important people, singing for them as her mother once had.

But as she grew older, the idea of distinction and superiority lost its appeal.

The quiet dignity of a lady of quality was significantly more alluring to Evelyn than any renown for her singing voice, but just as out of reach.

Her humming bounced from the hollow she sat within and echoed through the empty woods. Raising her head, she began to sing a song of larks and minnows that her mother had taught her as a child. It was silly and sweet, and the tune had always been a favorite of hers.

Letting her voice free, she enjoyed the unrestraint as she filled her lungs and sang the final chorus.

"I knew I did not imagine you, Lady Eve," a deep voice said to her left, startling her into sudden silence.

Jumping up, Evelyn backed against a thick branch, putting as much space between her and the man as possible. But when her eyes settled on the person hovering between two branches, his arms resting casually as he took a step up on a root and then onto the flat base of the tree, she gasped. How had he found her here?

"Your grace," she said at once, dipping into a low curtsy.

"So you remember me," he said, smiling.

They stood but three paces from one another on opposite ends of the tree. Evelyn leaned further back against a branch thicker than herself, her mind racing with the implications of the duke's presence.

"What are you doing here, your grace?" She'd wondered if it was him in the back of Lord Sanders' carriage, but had since convinced herself it was merely *Lord Sanders* whom she saw and her imagination had surely run away from her. She'd been thinking of the duke so often that the argument had held weight.

But no, the man was here. In this tree. With her.

His hair looked windswept, as though he'd ridden hard all morning.

But that could not be, for the ground was slippery with new snow. His eyes, however, were serious and resolute, watching her with directness. "I heard you sing and I followed the voice."

Drat her voice and her need to sing *loud*. Why couldn't she have simply been quiet? Well, because she had imagined herself alone. And nowhere near the duke.

"I don't mean in this tree, your grace. I mean what are you doing in Derham?"

His eyebrows lifting in bafflement, he focused on her. "I've come to stay with Lord Sanders, of course. I cannot believe my luck. Do you live nearby?"

His luck, indeed. Evelyn could not believe her own misfortune. Of course the duke would come to visit the very earl who owned these woods directly after she lied to him about her name. It was such an absurd coincidence that Evelyn wanted to laugh aloud as much as she wanted the earth to swallow her whole.

"I have come for the holiday," she said. Unease spread through her abdomen at her continued dishonesty. She should tell him now that it was a mere game she had played. That her lie from the masquerade was nothing more than a fantasy and she had taken advantage of the moment and the masks to say the words she'd dreamed of being true her whole life. She opened her mouth to do exactly that when Alverton stepped forward, hesitantly, and reached for her.

"Allow me to help you from that branch. You needn't fear me now that you've seen I am no poacher or gypsy."

Foolishly, no doubt, Evelyn placed her hand in Alverton's and held it tightly as she took a soft step down onto the base of the tree. They stood together on the center of the trunk, larger branches thicker than Alverton's waist reaching out in every direction and allowing them to feel as though they stood in a secluded, mystical place.

Time seemed to stand still. But she was proven wrong by the assumption that the world had stopped spinning when her breath clouded before her and dissipated.

"How could I have been so fortunate?" Alverton said, his voice a low whisper as his gloved fingers tightened around her own. "I came to the determination only last evening to seek you out on my return to London. Little did I know you were so close already."

She swallowed, pulling her hand free. "You are not making sense, your grace."

"I plan to court you, Lady Eve, if it is agreeable to you. I have not met a woman who arrested my attention so deeply as you have."

"You are mad, your grace," she answered, her lips tipping into a smile. He had known her for all of an hour. He could not wish to *court* her.

"I might be under a spell, if your voice is indeed magical," he responded, his voice husky.

Yes. She was correct. The duke was certainly disturbed.

He shook his head. "I realize how I sound. But I am not begging for you to marry me. Simply allow me to court you. To discover if we would suit."

"I am sorry, but I must refuse you. I cannot waste your time when I already know we won't suit."

"Why not?"

"Well," Evelyn began, swallowing her fear, "because I am not suitable."

He laughed, digging the humiliation further into her heart. His eyes were alight with mirth as he gazed down at her. "I shall not be put off, you know. I've been forced to endure the most ridiculous women for my mother's sake. I am finished with that business."

"I am in earnest," Evelyn continued, but the duke's unrelenting gaze forced prickles to run down her skin and she turned away suddenly, her own voice lost to the emotion of what could have been. Alverton wanted to court her and she had no choice but to refuse. The duke didn't want to court Evelyn, he wanted Lady Eve.

She needed to remove herself from his presence. Gripping the tree tightly, Evelyn lowered herself onto a tall root before hopping down onto the ground. Wind rustled by, teasing her with the scent of evergreen. She should be feeling the joy of the upcoming Christmastide, not the panic and disappointment of Alverton's company.

"Where are you going?" he called after her. But she set off toward home, not pausing to look back.

His footsteps were muffled by the snow as he jogged to catch up with her, but Evelyn did not slow. Finding the game trail which ran the width of the woods, she took it toward her house.

"Wait," Alverton called.

"No thank you, your grace. I must return."

"You would leave when I have requested you stay?" His tone of voice caused her to pause, but it was not a forceful, authoritative sound. Rather, he seemed confused.

Evelyn turned to find Alverton regarding her with curiosity. She could see that he felt rejected, and it was clearly foreign to him, just like it was the night of the ball. But she told him she was not suitable. Why could he not leave her be?

"Your grace," she began, soothing with her words as though he was a disappointed child. "This would not work. It would *never* work. Surely you can take my word for it and allow me to leave peacefully."

His eyebrows drew together, his arms hanging limp from broad shoulders. "I see. You are promised to another man."

Evelyn scoffed—she could not help it—and took a step back, bumping into a tree. She opened her mouth to deny the accusation when it struck her that Alverton had given her a perfect way out of the mess she'd entangled herself in.

As much as she would love to be courted by a duke, it was a ridiculous notion. She might have lied about her name, but she had not lied to him earlier about the state of her suitability. As a woman with no title or power, she was unfit to become a duchess. She *was* unsuitable. But the only way to make him believe it to be true was if she explained her lie. And her pride would not allow her to do so.

But a secret commitment to another man—however fictional he might be—was the perfect answer to her predicament.

"You are," he continued, shaking his head ruefully. "Of course you are. How did I not see it before?"

Guilt momentarily filled her body as Alverton glanced away, coming back to rest his gaze on her with disappointment.

"'Tis not widely known. And I beg you not to speak of it to another soul." She dropped her gaze to Alverton's boots before reaching his eyes once more. "Perhaps, your grace, we might part on good terms."

"Yes, of course," he answered, distracted. He glanced back over his shoulder toward the large tree and then sighed. "I am planning to remain with Sanders until Twelfth Night. Perhaps I will see you again over Christmastide."

"Perhaps," she lied. If it was in Evelyn's power, she would never see the duke again.

"May I escort you home?" he asked. "It cannot be safe to cross the countryside alone."

"Being found alone with you would be entirely more compromising, your grace. But I thank you for the solicitous offer."

He bowed, understanding resting on his brow. His bearing was stiff, his mouth set in a grim line. "Good day, Lady Eve."

Her stomach constricted as she savored the last time she would ever hear those glorious words. It was for the best, but that did not make it easy.

"Good day, your grace," she replied.

Turning away, Evelyn filled her lungs and did not empty them until she was well out of earshot. She could not allow herself to think of what could be possible if she was Lady Eve in truth. It would only make the situation more difficult to bear.

Approaching her house, she let herself into the warm kitchen and through to the dining room, where her brothers sat flanking her father, the three of them partaking of a hearty breakfast. They were just the sort of distraction she needed.

"There you are, you little mischief makers," she said, stepping forward and resting her hands on the table. "I was told this morning that you'd taken the horses out and went to fetch you."

Harry glanced up from his plate, an unrepentant expression on his face. "It was cold," he explained, "so we came back inside."

Evelyn chuckled, shaking her head. That certainly explained why she had not seen any hoofprints in the snow. "Finish your breakfast and then I shall read to you." Turning her attention to the older man, she said, "Father, have you any objection to my inviting the Coopers to dine with us on Christmas?"

He glanced up, his intelligent gaze reading her face.

"I have missed Julia deeply these last few months," she said, as if reminding him of her friendship with Julia would cause him to forget that Julia's brother was a doctor.

"No," he responded. "I have no objections to the Coopers. They shall make a fine addition to our Christmas dinner."

The smile which spread over her lips was wide and unrelenting. "I shall write to Julia at once," she said, turning on her heel.

"Do not get any silly notions," her father called as she left the room. She promptly pretended not to have heard him.

❄

DINNER THAT EVENING WAS QUIET. Aunt Edith complained of her headache through the duration of the meal and when they moved into the parlor following dinner, the older woman settled herself onto the chair beside the fire and moaned quietly.

"Can I get you another blanket, Aunt?" Evelyn inquired, crossing the room to retrieve a quilt from the trunk.

"Have you heard that Lord Sanders returned to Derham?"

Evelyn paused, her hands buried in the trunk. She was grateful to be facing away from the light of the fire to allow herself time to compose her expression. "Oh?" she said at length.

"Yes," Aunt Edith said crisply. "He's brought a man with him, though none of his family came."

Evelyn nodded, bringing the quilt to her aunt and laying it across the older woman's knees. "It should not affect us," she said.

"No," her aunt agreed, "it never does. But I did wonder…" The old woman trailed off, watching Evelyn through narrowed eyes. "Perhaps all is not lost yet."

Evelyn was afraid to ask Aunt Edith to clarify. The woman had a calculation about her eyes that was frightening. Swallowing her fear,

Evelyn straightened her shoulders. "Whatever plan you are forming, allow yourself to forget it at once."

She wanted to remind Aunt Edith that her marriage to Mr. Chadwick, while it did something to elevate her status, did not put their family on the same level as an earl. Lord Sanders was certainly not going to deem Evelyn worthy of becoming his countess—and neither would his houseguest, the duke.

"You underestimate me, my dear," Aunt Edith said, her voice eerie and low. "You are a gentleman's daughter, and do not forget it."

"Aunt," Evelyn said, doing her best to keep calm. "A gentleman's daughter is nothing compared to a Peer."

"We shall see."

CHAPTER 6

Even now, days after meeting Lady Eve in the grove of trees, Alverton felt like a simpleton for not connecting earlier that the woman he saw in the street was Lady Eve herself. Of course she was transposed to a different place—one would not expect a lady to be standing in the road on a cold winter morning—but he should have known her by her intelligent eyes. And he would have, he'd like to think, had he been able to see her eyes from the carriage.

She was, as he imagined, quite beautiful without the mask. It was difficult not to be angry at her for allowing him to dance with her when she was promised to another man. But alas, that was ridiculous and petty and he knew better. It did explain why she was so eager to deny his courtship.

His *courtship*. Alverton sat on the sofa in Sanders' drawing room and dropped his head into his hands. What a fool he had been. Lady Eve likely thought him mad for his quick request to call on her. He must have been out of his mind, for he hardly knew her. And a woman as beautiful as she with a voice so velvety and rich could not possibly be available. He had been wishfully thinking, that was all.

"Shall we ride into Derham on horseback or within the confines of a carriage?" Sanders asked, coming into the room and leaning against the door frame, his arms folded across his chest.

"Horseback, man. Always. I should like to see this hedge you spoke of."

Sanders lifted an eyebrow. "We might freeze."

"Doubtful." Alverton rose. "But either way, I am sure your vicar has a hearth warm enough to thaw us."

Sanders lifted his gaze to the ceiling and sighed. "If we do not melt in a puddle of boredom on his rug then we can liven our spirits again with a race back home afterwards."

Alverton stood and crossed the room, following Sanders to the front door where the butler stood waiting to help the men into their coats. "Why must we visit the man if it is bound to be so distasteful?"

"Good standing, I suppose," Sanders said. "We've always paid the vicar particular attention when coming to stay in Derham. His predecessor was my mother's brother."

"And this man?"

"It is difficult for him to travel," Sanders answered, understanding his friend's unspoken query. "We have no relation to Mr. Hart. We are following tradition."

"You have a much different tradition than we hold back home," Alverton said. He sucked in a sharp breath as the door opened and they stepped outside. The temperature had dropped once more and the frigid air made breathing difficult. "We make our vicar come to us."

"Yes, well, we might do the same. But our vicar can hardly walk."

Alverton paused on the walkway between the house and the stables and blinked. Sanders continued on through the snow and he hurried to catch up. "What do you mean?"

Turning to shoot Alverton a grin, Sanders chuckled. "You'll see."

They rode into town and stopped at the vicarage, sliding down from their horses simultaneously and tying their reins to the fence. Masculine tones floated through the door and it was clear the moment they approached the house that the vicar already had a visitor.

Alverton and Sanders exchanged a glance when the door swung

open and a man appeared, his sandy hair worn long and a well-cut coat upon his shoulders. "Oh," he said, surprised.

The vicar, Mr. Hart, approached behind the blond man—or so Alverton assumed, based on his walking unsteadily with the use of two canes. His hair was dark as night but he had the understanding eyes of a man of God. What surprised Alverton was his youth. For a man supporting himself with two canes, he looked to be a few years Alverton's junior.

"Alverton, meet our vicar, Mr. Hart," Sanders began.

"Ah, your grace. Lord Sanders," Mr. Hart said, bowing as best he could manage. "Please allow me to introduce Dr. Cooper, our neighborhood surgeon."

The men all bowed to one another and proper pleasantries were exchanged. "The other Dr. Cooper must be your father, I presume?" Sanders asked.

The man nodded, a pleasant smile on his lips. He had an easy way about him that inspired confidence. "Indeed. Though presently he's retired to Bath with my mother."

"In search of a remedy?"

"Yes," Dr. Cooper said. "For his gout."

Sanders chuckled. "How poetic." He turned to Alverton and explained, "The senior Dr. Cooper was also a doctor. He saw my father on occasion and I remember him well."

Dr. Cooper grinned. "I tried to tell my father he could recover just as well here as he could in Bath now that I am trained to take over for him, but he would have none of it. In truth, I believe he would not quit working while there was a need. So he has gone to Bath more for peace than the waters."

Sanders nodded. "An industrious man, I presume."

"Very," Mr. Hart said, nodding. "Dr. Cooper is a fine man. His son is, too."

One would think that the vicar, Mr. Hart, with his fatherly disposition, would be surrounded by children of his own. But he was unmarried, according to Sanders, and lived quite alone. His deformity of the legs, while strange, was not gruesome. And though the earl had told Alverton that the vicar was a dead bore, he seemed a nice sort of man.

Why were the men of Derham all young and unmarried?

Alverton glanced behind him as though all the old, married men of Derham were standing in the garden, but it was empty.

"Well, I shan't keep you," Dr. Cooper said, lifting his hat. "Your grace. My lord." He glanced back to Mr. Hart with an amused smile. "And my vicar."

"Good day," the men chorused behind the young surgeon as he walked away. Pleasantness aside, he was not the man Alverton would choose to send for if he became ill. Could Dr. Cooper really be qualified? He must not be over five and twenty.

"Please come in," Mr. Hart said, stepping back to allow space for Sanders and Alverton to file inside. The vicarage was small but warm and they took seats on a sofa as a maid bustled into the room bearing a tea tray.

Alverton could see at once why Sanders kept up with visiting the vicarage. The man walked slowly, heavily using the canes as he dragged one leg as though it was nothing more than dead weight. It was unpleasant to watch and Alverton glanced toward the window to allow the vicar privacy as he crossed the room and lowered himself gently into a chair near the seated men.

"You appear to be well," Sanders said, nodding unashamedly at the man's leg.

Alverton swallowed his shock as the vicar nodded, his eyebrows raised. "I owe a lot to the young Dr. Cooper. The man has used some unorthodox methods with my leg, but they've worked wonders. I cannot imagine I'd be walking at all if not for his influence."

Sanders nodded. "If he's anything like his father, then I am sure you're in good hands."

"Enough about me," Mr. Hart said, his eyes glittering with interest. "I have heard many tales about you since your last stay, Lord Sanders, and I have been dying to know if it is indeed true that you…" Pausing, the vicar cast a side-glance at Alverton. The duke straightened in his chair, sure that this was the oddest beginning to a conversation he'd ever witnessed between a man of God and an earl.

"Do not fear the duke's censor," Sanders said, waving a hand at Alverton as though he was insignificant. "He will not mind. Please, continue."

Mr. Hart cast his gaze at Alverton and then back at Sanders. Lowering his voice, he asked, "Is it true you raced clear from Kensington to Hyde Park in your curricle? In the middle of the day?"

The grin which formed on Sanders mouth answered the vicar's question for him. "Indeed. And I won."

Mr. Hart laughed, slapping his leg. "I am impressed, my lord. I should like to hear the whole of the story if you are willing to share."

"So should I," Alverton added, surprised. "Why did I not hear of this escapade?"

"It was during the heat of the summer and you were off gallivanting with your grandmother in Bath, I believe."

"Ah." Alverton nodded. "Yes. We tried the waters ourselves. Nasty, too. Though Grandmother was not gallivanting; that would have been quite the spectacle to be sure."

Sanders broke into peals of laughter. "Too true. The duchess would *never* do such an undignified thing. She is far too elegant."

Alverton watched his friend snicker, taken slightly aback. What had Sanders meant by such a thing? Sure, grandmother was dignified. She was a duchess. It was part of her duty to set the tone and the example. *Everyone* looked up to the ducal families.

"Did you have a team of two, or four?" Mr. Hart inquired.

"Four," Sanders answered, turning on the sofa to better face the vicar. "They were prime, too. All four matched perfectly and I owe them my victory."

The men went on to discuss the finer points of the race while Alverton waved away the offer of tea and ruminated on the things which occurred that day that did not fit in with his line of thinking.

He was not an overly proud man, or so he liked to think, but the familiar way in which Sanders conversed so easily with his vicar and the town doctor was not how Alverton was raised to hold himself.

As the visit drew to a close, Sanders lifted a hand to stop Mr. Hart from rising. "We can see ourselves out. Do not tire yourself on our account."

"Much obliged, my lord." Mr. Hart turned his attention to Alverton and watched him with the intelligent, knowing eyes of a man who saw more than what was plainly laid before him. He seemed to see into Alverton's very soul; the feeling was quite unpleasant. "Have you any plans for Christmas, gentlemen?"

"We will feast," Sanders said at once. "But my family is in Cheshire visiting my aunt and it will only be the two of us. A quiet repose that we are both looking forward to, in fact."

"Then I shan't burden you with an invitation," Mr. Hart said with no ill-will. "I am to dine with Mr. Trainor and his family anyhow. I suppose it would be awfully rude to arrive with additional guests."

"That name rings a bell," Sanders said, standing over the vicar. Alverton waited patiently near the doorway, quite uncomfortable with the way their farewell had lengthened and stretched. "Do I know the man?"

"You share a property line so I would be very surprised if you do not."

Sanders snapped his fingers. "Ah. The small house on the other side of Sanders Grove."

Alverton perked up, his attention drawn into the conversation. Was that not where Lady Eve had gone after they met? Just to the other side of the grove?

"Wonderful family," Mr. Hart continued. "You are fortunate to have them for neighbors."

"That is good to learn," Sanders said. They bid their farewells and the men left the vicarage, making their way onto the street to prepare to ride back to Sanders' house.

Alverton sucked a breath in between his teeth and blew it out with force. "Strange visit," he said.

"He is a good man," Sanders replied, his tone edged in defense. "Unusual, perhaps, but good."

"I am sure," Alverton agreed, good naturedly. They untied their horses and mounted them smoothly.

"Though I had not expected such an interesting conversation. The last time I called we spoke of nothing but sermons and the Sabbath. Well, I've one more call to make," Sanders said, "but if you'd like to avoid it, I understand. I must leave a card at the Hollingsfords, but I cannot know if they will be at home or otherwise detained."

Alverton was familiar with this family and, in particular, their daughter. If he was presented with a choice to avoid a visit, he would undoubtedly take it.

His friend knew him well, however, and a knowing smile lit Sanders' face. "You know the way home, I assume?"

Alverton nodded and the friends took off in separate directions. The country life was nothing if not gentle and relaxed, and it suited Alverton just fine. It was a good medium for determining what he should do to direct the course of his life when the holiday ended and he returned to London.

He felt as though he was stuck in an in-between. He knew he needed to wed, but there were no women who had appealed to him, short of Lady Eve. But he must remove her from his mind forthwith.

'Twas easier said than done, however.

Turning the stallion onto the lane which led to Chesford Place, Alverton pulled the reins, halting the horse reflexively.

Lady Eve stood in the road just a stone's throw ahead of himself and Alverton knew the moment her startled eyes reached his that he was at a metaphorical crossroads and the choice he made in that moment would affect him for long after. He could lift his hat and command the horse to walk on, or he could greet the lady.

And in that moment, he wished to speak with her.

Sliding down from his horse, Alverton took the steed by the reins and crossed the distance in a few long strides.

She looked lovely with her pink-tipped nose and rosy cheeks, her head bundled in a bonnet and a warm cape wrapped securely around her. A basket hung from one hand, showcasing leather-encased fingers and Alverton swallowed before bowing to her.

"Good day, my lady."

Her curtsy was elegant and quick. Why was she walking on such a cold day? And where was her maid?

"Good day, your grace," she replied. She glanced behind him to the road and swung her basket between both of her hands as though eager to continue on her way. Perhaps she felt uncomfortable now that Alverton knew of her engagement.

He could put her mind at rest, surely. "It is quite cold today."

"Yes," she agreed. "But exercise does much to warm one."

He wanted to ball up his fist and hit the tree just to his right. The weather? What an idiotic thing to mention. Of course it was cold. Both of their breath was becoming visible before their very eyes, mingling and dissipating in soft clouds above their heads.

And yet, he could think of no comfortable way to bring up her engagement. To gather more information.

"I am eager to be on my way, your grace," she said softly, dipping her head. "I am expected somewhere."

"Might I escort you?"

She looked down to the basket in her hand and then met his gaze. "I am afraid you would find it a tedious errand, your grace. I am delivering food to a family which has taken ill."

"Is that wise?" he asked.

She brought her head up, looking at him through slightly narrowed eyes. Was it confusion or annoyance which played on her face and formed small lines between her eyebrows? "They are mostly healed. I was informed that all of the fevers have broken. But the mother took ill and I am sure she is tired from caring for her children."

"Charity," Alverton replied with a curt nod. "How kind of you."

Lady Eve's cheeks darkened with a blush that made her all the more beautiful. "I am merely being a good neighbor."

He wanted to argue but held back, instead reaching forward for her hand. "Allow me to escort you," he said, surprising himself.

"But, your grace—"

"I cannot let you go alone now that I have crossed your path. So you will accept my help or leave me standing here uncomfortable and dissatisfied."

She dipped her head, but not before he noticed her small smile. He waited patiently until she shifted her basket and placed a gloved hand within his own. Squeezing her fingers, he laid her hand upon his arm and gripped his horse's reins in the other before turning the beast around and heading for town.

"I should carry that basket for you but then I would be unable to hold your arm," he said. "I am not sure I'm willing to give up the pleasure quite yet, so I shall be forced to act the cad."

"Are you always so flirtatious, your grace?"

"No," he answered at once. "In fact, I usually do my utmost to avoid the act of flirtation in every sense of the word."

"Then am I to be an exception?"

"It is apparent," he said, casting her a look, "that you are quite the exception, indeed. Now tell me of this family we are to visit."

"I should much prefer you remain hidden behind the brick wall before their house and allow me a minute to drop the basket in their kitchen. I will not be longer than a moment, I vow."

"What sort of gentleman would I be if I agreed to such a scheme?"

Her words were soft and sincere when she answered. "You are a duke, your grace. You must."

"And you are a lady," Alverton countered. "What say you now?"

CHAPTER 7

*E*velyn should have said it right then: *but I am not a lady*. She opened her mouth to deliver those very words but the duke's kind, brown eyes peered down at her and she found she could not speak. Instead, she settled for changing the subject.

"Do you have plans for Christmas, your grace?"

"Yes," he said proudly. "My friend and I shall eat a feast and not concern ourselves with pleasing anyone but ourselves."

"That sounds like a holiday for bachelors."

"Indeed. We planned it to be so."

"But what of your mother? And your grandmother? I believe you were escaping them when we met, if I am not mistaken."

"They remained in London and I shall see them again soon. My uncle and his family decided to come to London so I am sure my mother has much to concern herself with and hardly notices my absence."

"Do you truly believe that?" Evelyn asked, lifting her face to watch the duke's reactions.

His gaze flickered to her and then back to the lane they traveled. "No. She is likely fuming that I've missed a superb opportunity."

Evelyn longed to inquire about the nature of the missed opportunity. She released Alverton's arm long enough to move her basket to the other hand, stretching her fingers as they walked.

"Please, allow me to carry your basket."

"It is not terribly heavy," Evelyn replied. "But I find it easier to manage when I alternate arms."

Alverton's eyebrow lifted as he stopped in the center of the lane, holding his arm out and waiting. Evelyn handed over her load and the man regarded her with surprise. "This is quite heavy. You might have passed it to me sooner."

"We are nearly there," Evelyn responded, starting forward again.

Alverton caught up quickly, his long strides overpowering her quick ones. They reached a small cottage before long and Alverton tied his horse to a post before joining her near the door. Evelyn looked at Alverton, indicating the basket. He clutched it firmly to himself and she shook her head softly, chuckling, before turning to knock on the door.

A small, dirty child opened the door, turning large, shy eyes past Evelyn and onto the duke. Evelyn crouched down to the level of the girl and said, "Is your mother home? We have something we would like to leave for her."

The child nodded, casting one last awed look at the duke before turning to lead them into the house. Evelyn followed, but Alverton hesitated at the threshold. She caught his gaze and sought to shoot him a look which told him that they would be in and out quickly, but he did not seem to be put at ease.

It struck her in that moment that any of these people could call her by her real name. Pausing, she knew a moment's panic before allowing her eyes to drift closed and inhaling a sustaining breath. At this point, there was nothing she could do about it. She must simply move forward and hope the occupants within the home did not.

"Mrs. Taylor," Evelyn said, stepping into the small, dark kitchen. "How are you feeling? I've brought you some hot soup and bread. And Cook has prepared some meat pies and apple pasties for the children, when they are up for it."

Mrs. Taylor sat in a wooden rocking chair with a baby in her arms.

Her face was pale and her eyes sullen—residual effects of the fever, no doubt—but she seemed to pale even further when Alverton stepped into the room.

His bearing and clothing were indicative of his rank. And while it was not overly apparent that he was a duke upon first sight, it was undoubtedly quite distressing to poor Mrs. Taylor to receive such a distinguished gentleman in her kitchen. Particularly when she was feeling so poorly.

Evelyn struggled to know whether or not to introduce Alverton, for she feared that the discovery of his rank would only cause Mrs. Taylor further anxiety.

A man stepped from the bedroom door behind Mrs. Taylor, closing it softly behind himself and saying, "They are both on the mend, Mrs. Taylor. I believe you have nothing to fear."

His voice was familiar, but it was not until he glanced up and caught Evelyn's eye that she recognized him. "Dr. Cooper, how good to see you, sir."

His face broke into an endearing smile, his eyes crinkling around the edges. He opened his mouth to respond when Alverton called out, "Well met, Dr. Cooper. You do keep busy, don't you?"

All eyes in the room turned to the duke, but he did not seem inclined to notice.

"I like to keep tabs on those who are under my care, your grace," he explained, bowing.

The room came to a still as the ducal form of address settled upon the occupants' ears and Mrs. Taylor's face turned ashen. While some might have thought it an express privilege, this woman was clearly distressed. Evelyn knew at once that the best thing she could do for the woman's health was to remove the duke from her kitchen forthwith. Dr. Cooper seemed to come to the same conclusion and their eyes caught, which pushed them into simultaneous action.

Taking the basket from Alverton, Evelyn set it on the table. "I am afraid we must be off, Mrs. Taylor, but I am so glad to hear you are doing better. Please keep the basket. I hope the pasties are to your liking." She offered the woman a smile. "And there is a special treat for the children for Christmas," she added, thinking of the round, juicy oranges she tucked in the bottom.

Evelyn turned around and ushered Alverton toward the door, allowing him hardly enough time to dip his head in acknowledgement before she got him outside. She could hear Dr. Cooper speaking inside the house, though his voice was muffled through the door.

"I had not expected…" Alverton began. He turned away and scrubbed a hand over his face, breathing a sigh. Evelyn longed to hear his thoughts but waited patiently for him to collect them.

The door creaked open behind them and they turned in unison to find the same small, dirty child standing in the doorway, her solemn face peeking up at the adults with shy reserve from behind stringy, brown hair.

"Good day, Mary," Evelyn said, leaning down and resting her hands upon her bent knees. "Did you wish to come and meet my friend?"

The little girl nodded, stepping from the house and closing the door behind her. Evelyn reached forward and Mary slipped her tiny hand in Evelyn's, looking up at the duke under her lashes like a smitten debutante.

Evelyn looked to Alverton for approval and found his serious gaze resting on her. He watched her intently and her nerves rose accordingly. "Mary," she said, focusing her attention on the child, "do you know what a duke is?"

"A very important man?" Mary asked, her petite nose scrunching up.

A small smile lit Evelyn's lips and she nodded, reaching forward to tuck Mary's hair behind her ear. "Yes."

Mary leaned closer to Evelyn. Her gaze did not leave Alverton as she whispered, "Is he a duke?"

Evelyn nodded, and Mary's eyes widened. Hazarding a glance at Alverton, Evelyn was pleased to find a comfortable smile resting on his face as well.

"When you address a duke, Mary, you call him 'your grace.' Would you like to greet the duke?"

Mary nodded, looking up into Alverton's face with equal parts fear and excitement in her eyes. Evelyn could not help but smile at him over the theatrics of the situation and found him looking down at her again with a curious glint in his eye. His dark eyebrows were drawn together, and he watched her closely, causing prickles to run down the skin of her spine.

Clearing her throat delicately, Evelyn turned back to Mary and whispered, "You may tell him 'good day, your grace.'" Straightening herself, Evelyn stood. "Your grace, allow me to introduce Miss Taylor."

He dipped his head, bowing to the young girl. "Good day, Miss Taylor."

Mary smiled bashfully before dipping her head in response and saying, "Good day, my grace."

Evelyn turned to catch Alverton's amused eye and decided at once not to correct Mary. Turning her small face into Evelyn's leg, Mary giggled and then ran back into the house, nearly knocking Dr. Cooper over on his way outside.

He lifted his hat to Mary as she passed, but she did not seem to notice the doctor in her flurry of motion and the door closed quickly behind his back.

"Well," Dr. Cooper said, his eyebrows raised, "she has certainly overcome her illness, has she not?"

"That appears to be a safe assessment," Alverton agreed.

"A sweet girl," Evelyn said, turning to Dr. Cooper. "And the other children will recover quickly?"

"In time for Twelfth Day, if not Christmas."

"Christmas is tomorrow, sir," Evelyn reminded him.

He nodded. "And I believe we are dining at your house if I remember correctly. I feel as though I am constantly coming and going, so you must forgive my inattention. It would do me well to better know my own social calendar, but I am often concerned with other, equally important matters." He dipped his head toward the Taylor's rundown house. "But I am so pleased you have returned, for Julia's sake."

"You did not forget our dinner, sir, so I believe I must count myself fortunate."

Dr. Cooper smiled warmly. "I could never forget a social engagement with you, my dear."

Alverton cleared his throat and Evelyn turned to find him watching them closely, a grim set to his mouth.

"Forgive me, your grace," Evelyn said. "Have you met Dr. Cooper?"

"Yes," Alverton replied briskly, turning his attention to the doctor. "I had that pleasure just this morning."

"One would expect a town this small to be uneventful in regard to their medical needs. But no," he said in a self-deprecating manner, "the need for my assistance does not seem to wear down."

"We must count ourselves fortunate that you've chosen to stay then," Evelyn said. Dr. Cooper opened his mouth to respond, but then his gaze flicked toward the duke and he shut it again. Instead, he made a grunt of agreement and nodded accordingly.

"I must be off," Dr. Cooper said, running a hand over his hair and then replacing his hat. His sand-colored hair was cropped shorter than usual, but it made him look more distinguished. He'd always been a pleasant man, but now he looked handsome.

"Please give my regard to Julia," she said. "I look forward to seeing you both tomorrow."

Dr. Cooper reached forward and grasped Evelyn's hand. Bringing it to his lips, he bestowed a feather-light kiss on the top of her knuckles and said, "As do I."

Evelyn did not know what to think about the exchange. She brought her hands together, rubbing the area where Dr. Cooper—*Jared*, of all people—had kissed her hand with intent. But…intent for what, exactly?

"Friendly chap," Alverton said under his breath after Dr. Cooper had walked away.

Turning toward the horse Alverton had tied up, Evelyn waited for the duke to retrieve the reins and begin walking. "Yes, well, I've known the Coopers all my life."

The fact hardly explained Dr. Cooper's familiarity. Evelyn wanted to shake out her hands and remove from them the feeling of his lips. The spot continued to tingle, but she did not want Alverton to know that it bothered her. Instead, she clasped her hands behind her back and asked, "Have you regretted leaving London now that Christmas is only tomorrow? You shall miss spending it with your family."

"No," he said at once. "As long as my cousins are in London then I am pleased to be away."

"They are that tiring?"

Alverton guided Evelyn onto the road where he had first come upon her. He eyed her as though he was determining how much to share, and then said, "My oldest cousin is a title-chaser and has determined to set me as her prize. I would do well to avoid her until either she has wed, or I have."

Evelyn paused on the road and looked up at the tall man. The cold air began to bite at her and she shivered. "What a horrible thing to live through. Perhaps it is well that you've come to hide in Derham."

He chuckled, a warm sound that ran through Evelyn like honey. "I suppose I have come here to hide, haven't I?"

Did he expect a response? Evelyn turned back for the road and Alverton fell into step beside her. "But in truth, it matters not where I go," he said. "There are women everywhere who would make themselves ridiculous for a chance to snare the duke." He sighed, his face trained toward the road they walked on. "They all lie and exaggerate and puff themselves up, pretending to be whatever it is they believe I want them to be. It is difficult to know who I might trust."

Evelyn froze, though her feet continued to carry her along the road. She was afraid to look at the duke for fear that he would read her panic and realize at once that she'd been untruthful herself. Perhaps if she merely explained right now and came clean about the whole of it, he would understand her motivation and realize she had only meant it for her own pleasure. She had only lied about her name because she wanted to know what it felt like to be called a lady.

"What these women don't realize, however, is that the title bears a magnitude of responsibility that takes a great deal of strength and fortitude to withhold. It is not for the weak of spirit or mind, and certainly not for the lowborn misses who would corner me in a billiards room and attempt to be caught alone."

He spoke from experience, it would seem.

His words, full of disdain and contempt, frightened Evelyn and she resolved to take her secret with her to the grave. There was no possible way she would be able to explain now that she had merely wished to be called a lady, not when Alverton expressed such disgust for the *lowborn misses* who attempted to make something better of themselves.

She felt foolish to the extreme. Humiliation snaked through her and she sought for a way to alter the course of their conversation.

"Perhaps you might be interested in hearing that Derham doesn't have much in the way of social activities."

Alverton shot her a glance and she snapped her mouth closed. What had she been thinking? A duke as high-minded as Alverton would never stoop to town assemblies anyway.

"Not that you would attend them, if they did, your grace," she added. Alverton's smile was amused and Evelyn wished she hadn't spoken at all.

"Sanders has plans for the duration of our stay and I am fairly certain none of them involve leaving the estate."

"Except for right now," Evelyn said as hoofbeats clopped behind them and Lord Sanders rode into view. At least, that was who she assumed the man was. She hadn't laid eyes on him since they were children, his visits growing more infrequent as he aged. And when he did come, he did not stoop to visit the Trainors.

"Finished already?" Alverton inquired.

"Already?" Lord Sanders said, laughing. "Gads, man. I was there for an hour at least." He turned his attention to Evelyn and she swallowed.

"Do you know Lady Eve?" Alerton inquired.

"I don't believe I do," Lord Sanders said from high atop his stallion. He slid down and landed on the ground with a graceful thud. Lifting his hat, he bowed lower than Evelyn deserved. "My pleasure, my lady."

Unease slithered through her and she curtsied. "The pleasure is mine, my lord." Acute discomfort forced her hands to shake with nerves, and Evelyn glanced between the men. "I am afraid my aunt will wonder where I've gone off to. If you'll excuse me, I must go."

The men bowed. Alverton looked as though he wished to speak, but Evelyn did not pause long enough to allow him the chance. She spun on her heel and took off for the deer path through the grove.

By the time she was safely ensconced in the woods, she could hear two sets of horse hooves thundering softly past on the frozen ground. She slipped behind a tree and leaned her back against it, peeking behind the trunk to watch the men disappear down the lane which would lead them to Chesford Place.

Alverton glanced over his shoulder just before they disappeared, his gaze searching the tree line. He found her, and his eyes locked on hers for a moment before he was gone.

Evelyn squeezed her eyes closed, her chest rising and falling quickly with adrenaline. This lie was growing steadily and it was not good. Lord Sanders was her next-door neighbor. What if he recognized her when she was with her father or brothers? What if, sometime in the future, Lord Sanders saw her at church and addressed her by her fictitious name?

She'd gotten lucky at the Taylors' house, but someone was bound to call her by her correct name in front of the duke eventually.

That was it. She had no choice. She *couldn't* continue to keep the secret; it was not practical. Regardless of Alverton's earlier words, she had to come clean.

CHAPTER 8

"Do you know a poor family in Derham by the name of Taylor?" Alverton asked, leading his steed into the barn.

"Can't say that I do," Sanders replied, sliding from his horse. They handed their reins to the stable servants and crossed the snowy lawn toward the house. "Should I know them?"

"I should say not," Alverton said with feeling. He'd lived a comfortable life, and he was aware of his elevated status. But that was why he had never been forced to endure the filth which the Taylors lived in. And he was not meant to endure it, or he would have been born to a lesser station. "I had the unfortunate experience just today with Lady Eve. I escorted her to deliver a sick basket and I have to admit that it was highly unpleasant being in their house."

Sanders watched his friend from the side with an arrested expression. "What was so disturbing about the Taylor household?"

"The filth. Their poverty. Never in my life have I witnessed such squalor, and I have gambled in some questionable places in London."

"Perhaps it is good to see how these people are living."

"For what purpose? These are not my people," Alverton said, following Sanders up the steps and into the house.

Alverton's thoughts traveled back to his own childhood and the small shack in the village near his own home which housed a young boy he used to play with. The boy lived in a house much like the Taylors', and when Alverton's father had come upon them climbing trees one afternoon the duke had immediately forbade the connection and sent the other boy home. He had proceeded to teach Alverton the importance of sticking with those of his own rank, for he was born into the place he was meant to be.

And now, his chest panged. Alverton had felt the goodness of Lady Eve's charity, but she needn't have gone *herself* to accomplish her task. She could do the same good through a servant and save herself from exposure to the Taylors' poverty.

Though he had to admit, the child who had called him *my grace* was rather charming.

Warmth from the house enfolded him and he immediately crossed to the study and lowered himself into a chair before the fire, his friend following close behind.

"But does it not benefit you to understand others from every status?" Sanders continued. He seemed unable to let it go. "Though we need not struggle how they do, witnessing their hardship allows us to better appreciate our own blessed lives."

Alverton paused, attempting to read Sanders' sincerity. Had his friend gone mad? When had he ever cared about appreciating his own fortunes in this manner? Alverton appreciated his own just fine while he sent his servants about administering charity for the tenants under his care.

But Sanders appeared determined. "I do what I can for them. Though I admit I could do better."

"This is not your estate," Alverton argued. "This was your mother's."

"And the people mean a great deal to her because of that," Sanders said. "Even if she chooses to remain closer to our family seat. The steward still sends her reports of the work we do within this parish."

Alverton had a thought. He leaned his head back on the chair and smiled. "Tell me, what was the name of the grove prior to your father renaming it after himself?"

Sanders chuckled. "It was merely referred to as 'the grove' before that. I suppose my father did not like that it went without a name. But enough about this nonsense. I've invited Dr. Cooper and Mr. Hollingsford over for dinner and cards the day after tomorrow."

Alverton groaned. He was not sure if his assessment was correct, but after watching Lady Eve with Dr. Cooper, he was nearly positive the doctor was the man she had an arrangement with.

But how could it be? Her, a lady, and he, a mere country surgeon? Alverton shook his head. He *must* have misread the situation.

"I can see you resent the prospect," Sanders said apologetically. "It will not be all bad. Hollingsford might be a pompous toad, but Cooper is a good sort."

That was precisely opposite to the way Alverton felt at present. And he hardly knew Hollingsford above a few short encounters in Town.

"And," Sanders continued, "I was able to put off a dinner invitation at the Hollingsfords' home due to this dinner."

"Then I heartily approve."

Sanders chuckled. "I figured as much. Now are you going to tell me about the woman?"

Alverton glanced up quickly to find Sanders watching him closely. "No," he said. There was nothing to discuss. Especially with Lady Eve's unavailability.

"I saw the way you looked at her, man," Sanders said, his eyebrows raised. Stretching forth his legs, he crossed them at the ankles and leaned back, settling into his chair. "You have not so much as glanced at a woman on purpose in the last year."

The last year. Precisely.

"And I am not glancing now, either. She is not…" Alverton stopped himself. To speak further on the subject he would need to tell Sanders of Lady Eve's engagement, and she expressly asked him not to tell a soul. He would not break that promise, not even for his dearest friend.

"Yes?"

"Nothing," Alverton said. "I'm of a mind to shoot something right now. What say you?"

Sanders grinned. "I say yes."

※

THE WOODS WERE sparse but the dogs were able to rustle up a few birds, and Alverton shot at them with all the pent up energy his previous twelvemonth had acquired.

"While I was at the Hollingsfords today I heard tell they are holding an assembly in the village for Twelfth Night," Sanders said. "Have you any interest in attending?"

Alverton looked at his friend as though he'd sprouted horns, but the man was simply inspecting his reloaded gun.

"It is not my first choice in entertainment, as you well know."

A sudden scream pierced the woods and both men paused, turning toward the sound. Alverton caught Sanders' eye when the scream sounded again, young and high-pitched as though it came from a child or young woman.

Their eyes locked and seemed to make an unspoken decision. Tucking their guns under their arms, they took off in a run toward the sound, Sanders in the lead.

Though he was nearly positive the sound came from a child, he could not be entirely certain. Alverton's stomach clenched as he ran, his mind racing with fear for Lady Eve's safety. She seemed to travel the width of Sanders Grove frequently and he did not know if there were gypsies nearby or wild animals.

Wailing sounded, breaking through his panic. It grew louder as the men neared the massive tree where Alverton had first seen Lady Eve within these woods, and to his great relief, the wails did not sound as though they came from a grown woman.

A bright patch of fiery red hair grabbed his attention. "Over there," he said, pointing to a small boy laying on the ground, crying out in anguish.

Alverton raced to the boy's side, kneeling on the damp, frozen ground. "Where are you hurt?" he asked.

The boy could not be above ten years old. His freckled face was screwed up in pain, his eyes squeezed closed.

"Did you fall?" Sanders asked from just behind Alverton.

"Yes!" another voice shouted from high above them, causing both men to look up simultaneously. Another red-headed boy sat directly above them on a branch, straddling it while his arms circled it securely. "He was trying to beat me to the top and fell."

"Can you get yourself down?" Sanders called while the boy on the ground cried out in pain once again, squeezing his eyes shut. "I have an errand for you and I need you to come down here directly."

There was a moment of utter silence when the boy in the tree seemed to watch Sanders with some reserve. Alverton chose not to waste time in that quarter as Sanders clearly had things well in hand, and grabbed the boy on the ground softly by the shoulders. His eyes shot open and registered Alverton at once.

"Tell me where you are hurt," Alverton said with the authority instilled in him as a man of superior rank.

"My leg," the boy said at once.

Ah, good. So he could talk. "And what is your name?"

"Harry," he replied.

Alverton released Harry's arms, moving down to investigate the injury of his leg. "Do you think you can walk?"

Harry shook his head and Alverton did his best not to show his concern when he noticed dark red blood leaking through the boy's trousers. He must have sliced his leg on the way down, but it did not appear to be broken. Turning back to look in Harry's eyes, he said, "I am going to lift you and carry you home while my friend sends for a doctor. Are you capable of directing me to your house?"

Harry gave an audible swallow and nodded his head. The boy could easily be a pale-faced redhead; it was not such an uncommon combination. But Alverton believed the degree of ashiness on Harry's face was more likely due to the injury he'd sustained and not the natural pallor of his skin.

Digging his hands underneath the boy, Alverton scraped his knuckles on the icy earth, catching a sharp object with his skin which caused his hand to sting. He lifted Harry carefully, ignoring his own pain the moment an expression of discomfort lit the small boy's face.

"Now where shall I go?"

"This way! Follow me!" The other little boy leapt from the base of the tree and into Alverton's path, eager, it seemed, to be of some use.

"Not so fast," Sanders shouted. "Are you familiar with Dr. Cooper's location?"

The boy spun, looking between Sanders and the direction of his house. "Yes."

"Then run for the man. Tell him what happened and where he shall find us."

A determined light shone in the boy's eyes and he set off at once in the direction of town.

"Brilliant," Alverton said, nodding to his friend. "Now Harry, tell me where I am to go. For you must know you weigh more than a bag of rocks."

Not that Alverton himself knew what a bag of rocks felt like, but he could assume.

Harry delivered a small smile before pointing in the direction the other boy had initially run. "That way."

Alverton set off at a rapid pace. Harry was small and carrying him was no great burden—Alverton had not taken all of those fisticuff lessons for nothing it seemed—but he was paling rapidly and the warmth from his leg was seeping onto Alverton's arm. That could not be good.

"Who is the other boy?" Alverton asked, hoping to distract Harry from his pain. They were clearly identical twins.

"My brother."

"And his name?"

"Jack."

Nodding, Alverton glanced at Sanders, who kept pace just behind him on the narrow game trail. "And what were you two doing in that tree?"

"Catching pirates," Harry said, as though this was a perfectly reasonable explanation. "But we were supposed to be gathering evergreen boughs for the hearth." He squeezed his eyes closed. "I am going to be in trouble."

The boy needed further distraction. "Do you know who that large tree belongs to?" Alverton asked.

"Lord Sanders. But the man is never around." Harry gasped as his foot caught on a tree branch and Alverton cringed.

"Lord Sanders' absence makes it acceptable to play on his land?" Sanders asked over the duke's shoulder. "Are you not frightened of being mistaken for poachers?"

"We've always played on the tree. The old Lord Sanders told my father he didn't mind."

That must have occurred before this child was even born. Alverton quickly added up how many years there had been since Sanders' father had passed away. There was no way this small child was twelve years old. Was he being dishonest?

"I have it on good authority," Alverton said, shooting Sanders a look over his shoulder, "that the *elder* Lord Sanders died many years ago."

Harry scoffed. "Well, I did not mean that he allowed *me and Jack* to play on the tree. Only that he didn't mind *my sister* playing on the tree."

Alverton was about to inquire what Harry meant by his words when they broke through the treeline and came before a squat, square house nestled in a small open valley right beside the grove. Its stone walls were punctuated by even, consistent windows and smoke billowed from the chimneys.

"Is this your house?" Alverton asked.

"Yes."

Sanders ran ahead of them, pounding on the door with zeal. "Let us in," he commanded. "Your boy is hurt."

The door swung open to reveal an aged butler with wide eyes. Alverton mounted the steps and swept inside, past the servant. "Where to?" he asked, his voice sounding worried to his own ears.

"This way, sir," the butler said, leading him down a narrow corridor.

Alverton opened his mouth to correct the man's mistaken form of address, but shut it again. What did it matter if the butler had wrongly addressed a duke? There was a bloody, injured child in his arms.

The butler led them to a library just down the hall and Alverton swept inside, crossing to a long, leather sofa on the far side of the room. Bending down, he laid his small bundle there, gazing into Harry's frightened eyes and willing the child not to look at his leg.

The steady clicking of a woman's footsteps could be heard coming toward the room and Alverton turned to find an aged, white-haired woman in a voluminous gown and satin turban sweep into the room.

He knew her at once, and her calculating gaze took in the occupants of the room and settled on Harry. It was Lady Eve's aunt.

"Mrs. Chadwick," Alverton said, rising and delivering a bow. "Harry has fallen from a tree and injured his leg somehow, likely on his way down. We've sent Jack for Dr. Cooper and they should be here quickly if the man was found at home and available."

Alverton rather doubted the doctor *was* available, the way he seemed to be all over the town at all times of day, but he thought it prudent to keep that particular thought to himself. Besides, even he could begrudgingly admit that the man was doing a service to the town of Derham to be so wholly at their disposal. Dr. Cooper certainly was not shirking his duties as the town doctor. He likely was not poor because of it, either.

"Very good," Mrs. Chadwick snapped. She crossed the room and tugged at the rope, causing a servant to enter moments later. "Fetch Hubert."

"He is away from home, ma'am," the maid said.

Mrs. Chadwick turned sharply toward the maid. "What do you mean he's away? He is never away."

"He has gone into Derham, ma'am. He took the carriage just an hour ago."

Mrs. Chadwick's face pinched, the apples of her cheeks glowing red. "Well, fetch Ev—"

"What is it? What happened?" Lady Eve burst through the doorway, not bothering to cast her glance upon anyone other than the small child on the sofa. She knelt on the floor, picking up Harry's hand within both of hers and squeezing it as though in prayer, her elbows bent and resting Harry's hand under her chin. "Harry, do speak to me."

"It is nothing," Harry said, his voice weak and small. "I needed to get into the branch to chase away the pirates."

"I *told* you I would be your damsel, but you were to give me one hour to read first while you fetched the branches for decorating. Why couldn't you have waited one hour, Harry?"

"We did wait," he argued. "But the pirates came anyway, and we had to fight them off."

Lady Eve looked annoyed. "But you decide when the pirates come. Could they not have come in an hour's time?"

"Pirates don't wait for Lady Eve," Harry said. "They wait for no man."

CHAPTER 9

*E*velyn's face flushed hot and she pierced Harry with her gaze. She allowed the boys to call her Lady Eve when they played, for they were in agreement that surely a pirate would be far more interested in capturing a lady than they would a plain woman. But she had not anticipated Harry using the name outside of Sanders Grove.

She certainly did not expect to hear him say such a name before the duke and Lord Sanders, or Aunt Edith. But she could not deny her relief, either. She could only hope Aunt Edith hadn't noticed.

The front door slammed, and deliberate footsteps rang through the corridor followed by a pattering of lighter ones. Dr. Cooper stepped into the library with Jack on his heels and cut across the room unceremoniously to stand before the sofa.

"Harry," he said, smiling down at the boy. "Have you gotten yourself into some trouble, young man?"

"Yes, Dr. Cooper," Harry said, his voice soft and small. "It hurts something fierce."

"Where does it hurt?" Dr. Cooper asked, but even as he said the words his gaze traveled to the blood seeping from Harry's leg. Turning toward Evelyn, he said, "Will you call for rags and boiling water?"

She stood at once, and a hand came to rest on her shoulder. She did not need to turn to know that the large, strong hand which gripped her belonged to the duke. Alverton released her, pulling his hand back as he said, "Stay. I will go."

Evelyn nodded as Alverton spun away, Jack following behind him like a faithful hound, and she turned back to see Dr. Cooper pull a pair of shears from his black leather bag and begin to cut at Harry's trousers.

"What can I do?" she asked.

Dr. Cooper did not remove his gaze from his patient's leg. "Are you squeamish at the sight of blood?"

"I don't believe so," she said. She'd seen her father's hunting dog receive a wound from an angry fox just last winter and the blood which the hound had gotten all over the library rug had not bothered her in the least.

"Then come up here by Harry's head and distract him," he said in a low voice, indicating the other side of the couch. He turned and addressed Lord Sanders as Evelyn crossed behind him. "Will you escort Mrs. Chadwick away, my lord?"

Sanders nodded, offering his arm to Aunt Edith and leading her to a set of chairs on the far side of the room.

Taking hold of Harry's hand once again, Evelyn looked down at his sorrowful eyes and did her best to remain strong. "Will you tell me how this occurred?" she asked.

"I fell from a high branch," he said. "My leg scraped something on the way down, but I don't know exactly what happened. It was all so quick."

"I am sure Dr. Cooper will discover the depth of your injury right away and take care of everything. You may squeeze my hand as much as you please."

Heavy footsteps brought Alverton back into the room, Jack on his heels once again. Evelyn glanced over her shoulder, catching the duke's eye. His brows were drawn together, serious and concerned. He seemed to speak to her through the depth of his gaze, but she hadn't the slightest inclination what he was trying to convey. He crossed the floor and she watched his sure, steady stride as he flung the drapes further open and allowed more light into the room.

Dr. Cooper glanced up. "Thank you, your grace. That is much better."

Alverton grunted, his boy-shadow remaining close beside him.

Harry cried out and Evelyn squeezed his hand on impulse. A whimper caught her attention and she looked up to find Jack's terrified, sorrowful gaze. She wished at once that the boy was far away, and she there to comfort him. But she could not be two places at once.

Alverton must have sensed the urgency in her expression, for he said, "Do not worry, my lady."

Dr. Cooper halted, casting Evelyn a curious glance before returning to his work. A maid entered the room with the requested supplies and set them near the surgeon as Alverton led Jack to the area on the far side of the room, seating him beside Aunt Edith at an angle where he would be unable to watch Dr. Cooper as he worked.

Alverton must have realized, as Evelyn knew, that Jack would only leave the room at this point if he was dragged forcefully away.

She glanced to Aunt Edith, but the woman was likely out of earshot, her attention focused on Lord Sanders. Perhaps Aunt Edith was too far away to hear clearly, or too distracted, for she did not appear to have noticed the duke's use of her false name.

"My lady?" Dr. Cooper asked softly as he began to clean around Harry's wound.

"Shhh," Evelyn said quietly, bringing her attention back to her brother. She spoke softly through her teeth, though the murmuring of voices behind her indicated that the others were not paying attention anyway. "It is nothing. He is misinformed."

Dr. Cooper shot her another quick glance. "By whom?"

"That is not relevant at present."

Quiet settled between them for a length of time as Dr. Cooper wiped the blood from Harry's leg and then prepared the alcohol for cleaning the wound. "This shall hurt," Dr. Cooper said. "I would advise that you squeeze your sister's hand as hard as you can."

Evelyn prepared herself, firmly gripping Harry's small hands in her own. Dr. Cooper began pouring the liquid over the gash in Harry's leg and the boy screamed loudly, squeezing Evelyn's hand with all of his might. His hand went slack and she panicked. "I think he has fainted."

Dr. Cooper leaned over her, lifting Harry's eyelids. He sat back on his heels, confirming her fear. "It is not uncommon," he soothed. "And it will make this next part easier for him."

Evelyn caught sight of the needle Dr. Cooper intended to use to close Harry's injury and she shut her eyes.

"Miss Trainor—"

"Shhh!" Evelyn said, shushing the surgeon. "Why must you use my name right now?"

"Good heavens," he whispered back. "What else am I to call you?"

She grunted, looking to Dr. Cooper and widening her eyes. "It is not the ideal moment to hold this conversation."

"I beg to differ," he said. "You are in an ideal situation to explain this nonsense to me while the rest of the party is distracted."

He prepared to stitch Harry's leg closed and Evelyn squeezed her brother's hand, though he was likely unaware of her presence. "I met the duke at a masquerade in London before coming home and told him my name was Lady Eve."

"Good heavens, Evelyn. Why would you do such a thing?"

Dr. Cooper's shock was not comforting. She sighed. "Because I wanted to pretend it was real, I suppose. And I was absolutely convinced I would *never* see the man again or I wouldn't have done such a foolish thing."

"It was foolish, indeed," he scolded.

"Well, how could I have known he was going to come to Lord Sanders' estate?"

"If you were honest, it wouldn't have mattered," Dr. Cooper countered.

This she already knew, very well.

Dr. Cooper continued, his voice low. "What do you plan to do?"

She did not want to explain her actions to the duke, but it was evident she didn't have a choice. "I merely need to speak to him and explain myself. But I'd rather do so without an audience."

"Understandable," Dr. Cooper muttered. "Until then?"

"His grace thinks I am secretly engaged," she said, leaning slightly closer to the doctor. "And it is keeping him at bay."

She sensed Dr. Cooper freezing beside her. His hands returned to motion quickly but his face did not recover right away.

His voice lowered even further. "And who is the man he believes you to be engaged to?"

Evelyn shook her head. "It is a fictitious character. There is no one, Dr. Cooper, as you well know."

Understanding lit his eyes and he focused on completing his task. Soft murmuring sounded behind them and Evelyn picked out the deep, masculine timbre of Alverton's voice among the group.

It was a strange thing, having the duke in her father's library. She was just grateful Father was out on an errand and not home. His lack of title would give away her lie at once, and she wanted to explain herself before the duke found out on his own.

She blew out a breath of air. For such a horrible event, things seemed to be well in hand. Aunt Edith was not falling into hysterics, as Evelyn would have thought she would have done. But then again, she was being comforted by an earl and a duke—what more could the woman desire?

If only Evelyn knew the nature of Father's errand in town. He had been so secretive when Evelyn caught him outside and asked what the business was about. It was within his rights to keep personal matters to himself, of course, but she could not help but feel that he was hiding something.

She had *hoped* he was seeing the doctor. But with Dr. Cooper kneeling on the rug beside her, that was clearly not the case.

"What shall you do if your aunt refers to you by your name?"

Evelyn startled, her mind having been off on a different path entirely. "I suppose I must hope that she does not."

Evelyn's knees ached from her prolonged kneeling on the floor beside the doctor, but when Harry began to stir, she was excessively glad she hadn't risen to stretch her limbs.

"What is it?" Harry asked, his grumbled voice sleepy as his eyes began to blink open.

"You fell out of the tree, Harry," Evelyn replied softly. She sensed someone approaching, the soft thud of boots stopping just behind her. "Do you recall it? The pirates were infiltrating your ship and you had to escape on the planks. Or something of that nature. But you must have slipped and fallen. Dr. Cooper is here doing his best to mend your injury."

"And you shall be perfectly capable of fighting the pirates in just a weeks' time, Harry. A fortnight, perhaps, but no longer," Dr. Cooper said, his voice gentle.

Harry looked between them. His squinting eyes were understanding, but dulled—no doubt from the pain. "I was chasing the pirates, not the other way around."

"Of course you were," Evelyn agreed. "Now, should you like to remain here, Harry? Or can I call someone to carry you to your chamber?"

He swallowed once, anchoring his hands beside himself before pushing up to a seated position. The movement shifted his leg, however, and he cried out like a new kitten: soft, muted, but pained.

"I would be happy to move the boy," Alverton said, forcing the skin on Evelyn's neck to prickle.

She looked over her shoulder and was struck by the compassion in his eyes—something which had been missing when they saw to the Taylor family earlier. He nodded once, subtly, and Evelyn got to her feet, moving out of the way for Alverton to step closer.

Harry looked awed by the large man and allowed the duke to lift him carefully.

Evelyn turned, saying, "Jack, please show Alverton to the correct chamber."

Jack jumped into action, crossing the room quickly, his sorrowful eyes flicking between his brother and the duke. They left the room swiftly and Evelyn sank onto the sofa, still warm from her brother's tiny body.

Aunt Edith crossed the room to pull the bell.

"How might I be of service?" Lord Sanders asked, startling Evelyn. She glanced up and found his serious face watching her from across the room. She'd forgotten he was there.

Dr. Cooper cleared his throat, tossing the last of his implements into his bag. "I believe that is all, Lord Sanders. There is nothing to do at this point but wait for the boy to be back to climbing trees."

"But how did he cut his leg so?" Lord Sanders asked.

A small gasp escaped Aunt Edith, her eyes widening. She did not appreciate the vulgar talk, no doubt. Fortunately, a maid entered the room then and Aunt Edith was able to find distraction in directing her to remove the bowl and rags and to clean the area.

Lord Sanders crossed the room, coming to pause just before Evelyn. "Small boys tend to recover quickly," he said. "I only wish I could have been of some assistance. Alverton carried the boy all the way from the grove. I've done little more than shout for assistance."

He'd carried Harry all that way? "Thank you for your support, my lord," Evelyn said, rising from the couch. Aunt Edith shot Evelyn a telling glance before leaving the room. She chose not to read into the pointed look, for she hadn't the slightest inclination what the woman meant by it.

"Everything is well in hand here," Dr. Cooper cut in, coming to stand beside the earl. "You are welcome to return home to your visitors, sir. Harry's injury bled quite a lot, but it is not so deep as to incite panic at this point."

"My only visitor is with me," Lord Sanders replied.

"Forgive me," Dr. Cooper said. "There was a fine carriage turning toward Chesford Place and I only assumed you were receiving more visitors just in time for Christmas."

Lord Sanders froze. "Did you not recognize the carriage?" he asked, hopefully.

Dr. Cooper shook his head. "I did not."

Alverton entered the room. "Jack has remained with his brother upstairs. Sanders and I shall remove ourselves at once." He lifted his sleeve and Evelyn caught sight of the blood which covered a large part of the forearm of his coat.

Lord Sanders scrubbed a hand over his face. "That is wise. Evidently, we have visitors."

Alverton's eyebrows rose. "Who?"

Shrugging, the earl gestured to the doctor. "Dr. Cooper saw a fine carriage traveling to Chesford."

Ominously, the men exchanged glances. Evelyn longed to inquire about the depth of their disappointment, but refrained.

Lord Sanders bowed to Evelyn, saying, "My lady," and turned to go. She glanced up, sweeping the room at once and was grateful to find Aunt Edith still absent.

Alverton approached, his countenance grim as his gaze flicked between Dr. Cooper and Evelyn. "Please keep us apprised of master Harry's condition."

"Of course, your grace," Evelyn said.

Dr. Cooper bowed. "Thank you for your assistance, your grace. I am sure the family is quite grateful."

"Indeed, we are," Evelyn added. She could not believe a man so top-lofty and elite had carried her brother such a distance. Her eyes trailed his arms, his well-cut coat defining muscles she previously hadn't noticed.

But above the strength and stamina required for the action, Evelyn respected the strength of his character even more.

"It was nothing," Alverton replied. He reached for Evelyn's hand and she gave it to him readily, her breath catching as he placed a light kiss on the back of her knuckles.

Alverton held her gaze as he lifted his head, not sparing a glance for the doctor who stood beside her. She could feel the shift in the energy of the room at once and her breath came in shallow, quick draws. Her hand burned from the duke's touch and he released it. A cool chill swept her person as he stepped back and she dipped into a curtsy.

Dr. Cooper and the duke exchanged farewells and Alverton left the room in long, sure strides. A quiet fell over Dr. Cooper and Evelyn as they listened to the Peers' retreating footsteps.

"Who do you think has come to visit the earl?" Evelyn inquired, her gaze fixed on the open door.

"I can't know," Dr. Cooper said. "But I saw the silhouette of a woman in the window and she was not a woman I recognized."

"Old or young?"

Dr. Cooper was silent long enough to draw Evelyn's attention and she faced him, embarrassed to find his knowing glance watching her. "She was young. Younger than Julia, at least."

And Julia was near the same age as Evelyn. She took the hint to mean that the visitor was younger, more beautiful and certainly a higher rank than Evelyn's own. But perhaps that was her own fears manifesting themselves and not Dr. Cooper's intent.

He had merely said the woman was young, and nothing more.

Evelyn shook her head. Did it matter if the woman was eligible and here for the duke? No. It did not matter, for Evelyn herself was *not* eligible for the duke—not even close.

And besides, the woman could easily be visiting the earl. Or married.

"You are exceedingly distracted, my lady," Dr. Cooper said. "Allow me to take my leave."

She shot him a wry smile. "You must not refer to me in such an inappropriate manner."

"But if the men overheard…"

"They are gone. And I must end it, anyway. I have grown tired of the charade. It has drawn out entirely too long."

Lifting her hand in his own, Dr. Cooper squeezed her fingers. "Good day, Miss Trainor. I wish you luck."

With that, he left the room.

CHAPTER 10

The Chesford servants were scurrying about the corridors and up and down the large, curved staircase with purpose. Some carried luggage while others fastened evergreen boughs to the bannister and hung mistletoe above the entryway. Alverton stood beside Sanders in the main hall, listening to the activity and hoping with all his might that it was not due to visitors of the female variety.

"Where is my butler?" Sanders asked with disbelief.

The man appeared suddenly, causing both Alverton and Sanders to jump slightly.

"Do forgive me, my lord," the butler said, bowing. "I was seeing to your guests."

"Who are these guests?" Sanders asked. "I am not expecting anyone."

Clearing his throat, the butler looked at Alverton. The duke's stomach dropped. Oh, no.

"Her grace, the Duchess of Alverton has arrived with two women."

"My grandmother?" Alverton asked.

"No, your grace. Your mother. And she has brought a Mrs. Rowe and a Miss Rowe."

Alverton groaned, dropping his head back in frustration, and Sanders chuckled, clapping him on the back.

"I suppose I ought to greet my mother. Sanders," Alverton said, facing his friend, "I apologize. Heartily."

"Think nothing of it."

Alverton took the stairs to the guest chambers. He shrugged from his bloody coat, leaving it in his own room before following his mother's dignified, distinct tone to the correct chamber. Rapping his knuckles on the door, he stepped inside, relieved to find his mother surrounded by her own servants, but no one else.

He would put off seeing Miss Rowe with her cat-like smile and frilly curls as long as possible.

"Mother," he said, his tone just short of scolding.

"Do not come in here and scold me, child. I reserve the right to wish to see my son on Christmas day."

"And yet, you did not pause to consider that your sister might have wished to spend Christmas day with her own family?"

"Oh pish," she said, lifting her nose in defiance. "Cassandra desired to see her dear cousin, and who was I or my sister to refuse the girl? Such a sweet disposition. And so very refined in her manners."

Clasping his hands together behind his back, Alverton sought patience. "Mother, you must know—"

"Leave us," she said crisply, forcing each of the three servants to pause at once. They dropped the items they were unpacking, or the bedclothes they were arranging, and filed from the room, the final maid closing the door softly behind her.

Mother lowered herself onto a brocade armchair beside the hearth, indicating the seat beside her. Alverton obeyed, clenching his jaw to guard his tongue against lashing out.

"It is your *duty* to wed, Alverton. You cannot put it off forever."

"I do not intend to—"

"Allow me to speak," Mother said harshly. "I have done my best to examine and filter the debutantes. I pride myself in supplying you with a wonderful selection of women. It is not as though I am allowing each and every title-hunting tart into our drawing room. Allow me the decency of accepting that I have your best interests in mind. For I have not set out to destroy your life, but to enrich it."

"But my cousin, Mother? She is ridiculous."

She speared him with a glare. "Your cousin comes from impeccable lineage. She is refined and capable of taking on the duties involved in becoming the next duchess. If you would only look past yourself then you might see the potential that lies within this alliance."

Alverton fumed. He wanted to run from the room—nay, from the house itself—screaming at the world to leave him alone. But alas, that would make him appear as though he belonged in Bedlam. And he absolutely was not mentally unstable. He simply wanted to marry a woman who did not grate on his last nerve.

Was that really so much to ask for?

"Mother, I will say this one time, and I intend for it to be my last," he said, his voice low and dangerous. He'd caught her attention and he held her gaze as he rose to his full height, affecting his power and strength in exhibiting his size. She might be his mother, but he was still the duke. "I will choose my wife. No one but I will have a say in the woman I choose to wed. And you may warn Miss Cassandra Rowe that if she puts herself in a position to be compromised, she will suffer the consequences alone. I will not have a repeat of the scenario in the billiards room. And I will not marry the girl just to save her reputation."

Mother opened her mouth to speak but this time Alverton cut her off. "I promise to choose a woman of good breeding and social standing with the bearing and grace demanded of a duchess. But *I* will choose her."

After one final, solid glare, Alverton turned away from his mother and left the room, ignoring her groan of irritation. He sped down the stairs and outside. He did not care if it was quite literally freezing outside, he needed to get away from the toxic nature of the house and breathe.

❄

THE WOMEN who arrived utterly uninvited to Chesford Place were quite happy with the arrangements Sanders had made regarding Christmas festivities. They were more than happy to partake in a quiet feast without additional guests.

Alverton, on the other hand, was quite perturbed.

He stood at the top of the grand staircase as servants bustled about putting garland above the windows and tucking holly in the boughs. He listened to the women talk gaily between themselves through the open doorway in the drawing room and wondered where he ought to go to be away from them. It was Christmas Day. And he'd already had nearly as much as he could handle from his ridiculous cousin.

The day before, after running from his mother, he'd remained out of doors as long as his frozen limbs would allow and then begrudgingly took himself inside to change for dinner. The evening was spent ignoring Miss Rowe's coquettish glances and fluttering eyelashes and doing his best to avoid entering into conversation.

Mother, of course, had pouted incessantly. But Alverton decided that ignoring her childish behavior was not a chore.

He was positive dinner this evening was going to be much of the same, and the idea made his stomach churn in discomfort. A high-pitched peal of laughter escaped the drawing room, traveling up the stairs and forcing him to flex his arms to combat his irritation. Grasping the stair rail, Alverton contemplated returning to his room.

But, no. He'd hidden himself away there all morning.

And where had Sanders got himself off to?

The poor man had done more than his share of holding the conversation at dinner the night before. If he had escaped for a break, it was well earned.

Taking himself downstairs, Alverton sought out the footman who stood post beside the front door and asked, "Where might I find Sanders?"

"He's gone to see after young Harry Trainor, your grace."

Of course. What a perfectly good idea that had been. The poor boy had hurt himself the day before Christmas and was likely downtrodden and disappointed. If only Alverton had thought of it himself. Or, even better, if Sanders had invited him along.

He let himself outside and began walking toward Sanders Grove and the game trail which he now understood would direct him to the house where Lady Eve was residing. He was still confused about the composition of her family, and who she was staying with in Derham.

Her aunt, Mrs. Chadwick, hadn't been forthcoming the day before when Alverton subtly tried to question her on Lady Eve's family. He could not blame the woman, however, when Harry lay on a couch just across the room writhing and moaning in pain—that was, until he'd passed out, the poor boy.

The woman had been quite interested in Sanders, however, and had gone so far as to extend him an invitation to dine on Christmas day. Sanders refused, but Alverton had wished it would have been appropriate to accept.

Alverton cared very little that Lady Eve had formed an attachment with another gentleman. After the ordeal in her library with Harry's injury, Alverton was positive the man was Dr. Cooper. Given their familiarity and the proximity at which they had knelt beside the couch while the doctor administered to the boy, the two were clearly very close. Lady Eve deserved quite a bit more than the young doctor was prepared to offer her.

Alverton had talked himself into saying as much to Lady Eve. But then he had paused behind her and overheard her speaking to her brother about playing a game. Pirates, or some such thing. Her originality was refreshing and her love for her younger brother more than apparent.

And something about their interaction, coupled with her ease in the home of the Taylor family, forced Alverton to realize that perhaps there was more to Lady Eve than he realized. She was refined, graceful, beautiful and poised, and yet she spoke of imaginary pirates, took baskets of food to sick households, and did not faint at the sight of her young brother's leg being stitched together by a surgeon.

And that *voice*. Alverton groaned aloud, bringing his hands up and running them through his hair.

Lady Eve was incredible. She might have claimed an attachment to another man, but she was not married *yet*.

With renewed vigor, Alverton continued down the game trail toward Lady Eve's house. Birds were absent from the trees and the grove held a serenity about it which soothed him.

Which was partially why he was so utterly frightened when he turned on the trail and nearly ran directly into a woman standing still in the center of the narrow path with a cape around her shoulders and her face trained on the ground.

He recognized the cape. And her reddish-brown hair was the hair he'd spent quite a lot of time imagining in his mind.

"Lady Eve?" he asked. She looked to him, her face betraying red-rimmed eyes. The fact that she cried was further proven by a dainty sniffle and a subtle shake of her head.

Alverton stepped forward. "What is the matter, my lady?"

She laughed, though it was without humor. The sound frightened him, causing prickles to run down his neck. He stepped forward, reaching for her with one hand. "Please, tell me."

"I know I must," she said, her usually strong voice faltering. "I only wish it needn't be so."

Her ambiguity was not pleasant. He glanced around for a place to seat the distraught woman and eyed the large roots coming from the monstrous tree not far away. "May we sit?"

Nodding, Lady Eve took his arm and followed him to the tree, sitting on a root which jutted out in the perfect shape to form a small seat.

"It is my father," she said, sniffling once more. "I feel so utterly useless to assist the man. I know I can be of help to him but he simply will not allow me to do so."

"Assist him in what way?" Alverton asked, leaning against the trunk and folding his arms over his chest.

She sighed, using a handkerchief to wipe away stray tears. "He is ill, but I do not know the nature of what ails him. He refuses to confide in me. I wish for him to leave parliament and retire here, but he stubbornly refuses. And at what gain?"

"To make a difference in his country, I would assume."

Lady Eve glanced up, catching his eye and smiling faintly. "He has done enough of that, I presume. It is time to consider his health before he's taken from this world and my brothers left without a father."

Alverton nodded. She made a valid point.

"Who is your—"

"But would you truly like to know what bothers me?" she asked, cutting him off. Her eyebrows were drawn together in concentration.

She was lovely, even in distress.

"What is it that bothers you?" he asked.

She drew in a shaky breath. "I simply want him to trust me. If he would but explain the nature of his illness, then perhaps I might be able to be of some assistance. But, no. Instead, he entreats my aunt to come with us to London and do her utmost to find me a husband. He does not want my help, your grace. He wants me gone."

"But are you not engaged? Can that not be something which is easily attained?" he asked. Unless, of course, the man is unsuitable. Like, a doctor. "You needn't answer that," he continued. "Forgive my forwardness."

Lady Eve watched him a moment, her unwavering gaze forcing him to swallow. She rose, coming to stand just before him. There was hardly more than a hand's width between them and Alverton felt enlivened by her proximity. "I have not been completely honest with you, your grace."

A sudden thump sounded above their heads and Alverton looked up to find a small boy peeking over the edge of the tree.

"Jack, what on earth are you doing up there?" Lady Eve asked, exasperated.

"Nothing."

She turned toward the tree, her shoulder brushing Alverton's arm and causing warmth to race up his shoulder toward his heart.

Lady Eve stepped away. Had she felt it too?

"Jack, come down here at once. It is not polite to eavesdrop."

His small face fell. "But I was here first."

Silence sat between the siblings a moment. It was true. The boy had been there first.

"Come," she said. "Let us return home."

"I was on my way to inquire after your brother," Alverton said. "Will you be so good as to accompany me?"

Jack's eyes lit up and he scrambled from the tree. He'd been much like a devoted puppy the day before, eagerly following Alverton as the duke transported Harry. But it was all worth it for the gratitude which shone in Lady Eve's eyes. She took his offered arm and they set off toward the estate.

"You're wrong, you know," Jack said, skipping ahead of them. "Father did not ask Aunt Edith to marry you off so you would be forced to leave. He told her to find you a husband who could care for all of us."

Lady Eve paused on the path, her hand slipping from his arm. Alverton halted, turning back to see her grief-stricken look, eyes wide with fear playing across her face. Jack skipped ahead, running from the woods and toward their house.

Alverton reached for her hand, against his better judgement, and held her fingers tightly. "You do not know what he means by that. He is simply a father doing his best to care for his children."

"Why would it matter who I married if he did not fear his own demise?"

Alverton looked into Lady Eve's stormy, tearful eyes and did not have an answer for her.

She blew out a shaky breath and seemed to be working to compose herself. No matter how he tried, he could not remove his eyes from her. Her dainty features were pink-tipped and rosy, and he longed to reach forward and wrap her in a tight embrace.

It was an absurd notion, but he could not fight the feelings which arose of their own accord. He was very obviously developing feelings for this woman and it frightened him as much as it excited him.

"Who is your father?" he asked. "I must know him if he works in parliament, for I am heavily involved in Lords. Perhaps I might be able to do something to help."

She cast her eyes to the forest floor, shaking her head slightly.

"What is the matter?" Alverton asked. He tightened his hold on her hand, reaching forward with the other to lift her face softly by the tip of her chin.

Alverton tried to lighten the moment with a smile, but all it seemed to do was force Lady Eve to step back. Pulling her hand from his grasp, she created a barrier between them of palpable space, her gaze darting everywhere but his face.

"You are beginning to worry me, my lady," he said.

Her eyes squeezed closed and she shook her head. "No, do not call me that."

Call her by her title? Confused, Alverton stepped forward. Lady Eve's eyes shot open and she stepped back as well. Panic seemed to filter through her. "No. I am not…that is, I meant to tell you earlier, but I did not know how to say it."

He waited. Apprehension fell over him, and he watched the struggle play out over her face.

"I am not Lady Eve, your grace." Bringing her gaze up to meet his, she said, "I am no lady at all."

CHAPTER 11

He did not step away from her, but Evelyn could see the distance forming between them regardless.

"What do you mean, you are not a lady?"

She swallowed, doing her best to hold his gaze. "I am Miss Evelyn Trainor, daughter to Mr. Trainor of the House of Commons. I only told you I was Lady Eve because—"

"You lied," he said plainly. His face transformed to stone.

Evelyn nodded. "Yes, but only because I did not anticipate seeing you again."

Alverton took a step back, running a hand through his hair. "Did you not expect that I might find you interesting enough to pursue?"

"Of course not," Evelyn said, confused. What was this anger coming from? Of course he had a right to be upset, but Evelyn had told him the truth…this time. She had never intended to see him again after the masquerade.

"I am not a title-chasing woman, your grace. Is that not clear in the way I have done my best to *avoid* a connection with you? Surely if I was after your title, I would have leapt at the opportunity of being courted by you."

He shook his head, his eyes growing angrier. "Not if it gave up your ruse. You would have had to employ your household in the scheme." He paused, his gaze turning toward the direction of her house. "You did, didn't you? Your own brother referred to you as Lady Eve whilst he lay on the sofa yesterday."

"Because it is a game we've played since he was a very small boy. It is a game I have played my entire life with a dear friend of mine. But I can assure you I would never lie with the object of making it real, your grace. I do not desire the title, for then I would have to be married to a titled man." She must make him understand her motives. Regardless of her true feelings, it was important to force Alverton to understand that she did not desire him for a spouse—now or before. She sucked in a breath and spat her final blow. "And there is not a titled man of my acquaintance whom I could stomach marrying."

Alverton's already stone face hardened further, his eyes going dark. He raked his gaze over her person and stepped back. "Thank you for your *honesty*, Miss Trainor. I apologize for so wrongly using you." He paused a moment before continuing, "But how can I trust anything you say now?"

He did not offer her an opportunity to speak further, but turned and stalked away, toward Chesford Place.

Evelyn's chest heaved with adrenaline, her hands shaking from the confrontation. She immediately wished she could recall the words spoken in anger, for she did not mean them to be hurtful. She only wanted him to understand that her dishonesty had nothing to do with him.

But that was not true, was it? It was his desire to avoid title-hungry flirts which had forced her to keep the secret longer than she'd intended.

But what did that matter now? Groaning in irritation, Evelyn turned on the path and marched home. Given his extreme reaction, Alverton was likely going to do his best to never see her again. And to think, just minutes ago she had been hoping he would pull her into his arms and wrap her in a tight embrace.

So much for that ridiculous daydream.

Evelyn was so distracted by her own thoughts she hardly noticed the carriage rumbling down the lane until it stopped in front of her own house.

"Happy Christmas!" Julia called, drawing Evelyn's attention at once.

She glanced up to find her friend stepping from their carriage on the arm of her brother. Julia's head tilted to the side as she approached, her soft eyebrows drawing together. "What is it, Evelyn?"

Shaking her head, she said, "Nothing. My ruse is up and the duke is furious."

Dr. Cooper paused behind his sister, turning to search her eyes. Julia merely shook her head. "I was afraid of this. What shall you do?"

"Avoid him, I suppose. But I don't think that will be a hardship. He has determined that I am just the same as every title-hungry debutante who does their utmost to trap him in marriage."

"Then clearly he does not know you at all," Dr. Cooper said, offering his arm and a conciliatory smile. "Now let us go inside before we all freeze."

Evelyn led her friends into the house, but it was for naught. She was frozen to the core. Alverton's biting words and angry face would not leave her mind's eye, and she wondered if her heart would ever thaw.

❄

Christmas dinner had been quite the same as always. Julia and Dr. Cooper were pleasant company, the former keeping Father in conversation and the latter doing her part to visit with Evelyn and Aunt Edith both. Mr. Hart arrived, rounding out their numbers and conversation.

But Evelyn was far from pleasant that evening. She knew she was far more reticent than usual, but it seemed to escape her father. Aunt Edith, on the other hand, eyed her closely, suspicion gleaming in the older woman's gaze.

Sitting in the library, the Yule log blazing in the fireplace, the conversation turned to politics between the men, as it usually did when Father, Dr. Cooper, and Mr. Hart got together.

"When shall they learn to speak of those things when they are not in the same room as the women?" Aunt Edith complained. "It is always this way, and I find it so tedious."

"Then it is good we are here to distract you," Julia replied. "Did you hear of the new visitors at Chesford Place?"

"Only what your brother shared with us yesterday," Evelyn replied. "There was a fine carriage seen traveling toward the earl's estate."

"A fine carriage, indeed," Julia said, leaning closer. "Containing a duchess and two women."

"Alverton's mother," Evelyn said at once. But she saw him just that morning and he hadn't even mentioned it. "And who are the women?"

Julia looked between Aunt Edith and Evelyn. "I do not know this to be certain, but I was informed that one of the women is the duchess's sister, the other woman her daughter."

"But Alverton does not have any sisters," Evelyn said.

"Not the duke's sister, Evelyn," Aunt Edith snapped. "His cousin."

Realization dawned on her and she sat back in her seat, her fingers playing with the fringe of her shawl. It was no wonder the man had been on edge that morning—the very women he was hoping to escape had brought themselves to his doorstep. It was horrible how blatantly they did not seem to care about Alverton, the man, and merely sought Alverton, the duke.

And his own mother was part of it all.

"I invited them to dine this evening," Aunt Edith said, causing Evelyn to grow still. "But Lord Sanders claimed a prior engagement. Perhaps he already knew of their impending arrival."

He had seemed surprised to hear that a carriage was on its way to his house, but Evelyn supposed he could have been play acting.

Although, that did not seem right to her.

"I am sure I've never seen so handsome a man as Lord Sanders," Julia said, surprising Evelyn. She was usually so quick to blush, but her cheeks were not the slightest bit pink.

"Perhaps I ought to try again," Aunt Edith said, a hungry look in her beady eyes. "If we extend the invitation to include their guests, then surely the men will not refuse."

"A duke has every right to refuse condescending to dine in our home," Evelyn argued. She could not share the finer points of the development between Alverton and herself with Julia yet, for she did not want Aunt Edith to hear the details of what had transpired in the woods earlier, but she was certain Alverton would never step foot near her again.

Julia smiled at Aunt Edith with a level of patience Evelyn did not possess. "All the same, you are certainly welcome to try."

Aunt Edith pierced Evelyn with a look that caused trepidation to swirl within her. What was she planning? Surely she must realize they were born too low to reach for such heights. *Surely* she could not think chasing the earl or the duke a good idea.

Evelyn swallowed, turning her attention to her father. He was relaxed and in his element, his hands crossed languidly over his stomach and a satisfied smile peeking out from under his mustache. He did not appear ill or weak at the moment, but she could not let this opportunity pass. Perhaps if she was to mention something, Dr. Cooper would become interested enough to inquire further on Father's health.

For one small moment she considered commenting on the vicar's improved leg—for he had hardly been able to walk just earlier that year—as a way to enter into the conversation of health. But no, that would not be at all kind of her in such a setting. And the man looked peaceful, his dark hair pushed away from his face and a comfortable sense about him.

Clearing her throat, Evelyn garnered the attention of the entire room. Well, there was no sense in wasting the opportunity. "Shall I call for tea, Father?" she asked. "I know how *tiresome* evenings have become for you of late."

"Yes, dear," he said, and then promptly turned back to finish what he had been saying to the men.

Evelyn stood, watching Dr. Cooper as though she could speak to him through her mind. He caught her stare and held it, his fair eyebrows arching as though in question.

Evelyn widened her eyes, glancing to her father in an indication that Dr. Cooper should ask *why* the man was feeling so tired in the evenings, but the doctor did not seem to understand her plea. Frustrated, she turned away and pulled the bell, asking the maid who entered moments later for a tea tray.

She was certainly going to need to be more creative. Unless she could find a way to get Dr. Cooper alone, then she could speak plainly to him.

"Julia," she said, seating herself beside her friend once more on the couch. "How has your father been?"

"He is well," her friend replied. "He is enjoying Bath immensely and has reported that the waters are doing wonders for his gout. I do not know if that is truth, but I am glad he is feeling well."

"How wonderful. Surely he misses Derham, though. Does he plan to return?"

"For a visit, perhaps, but I do not think we will find him living here again."

"He was a good man," Aunt Edith said, decisively. She made it sound as though Julia's father had died.

Evelyn and Julia shared a glance, swallowing their mirth. A maid entered the room bearing a tray.

"Father has determined that he could not rest if he lived in Derham," Julia explained as Evelyn began preparing the tea. "And Mother enjoys the variety of Society. I am quite certain they will never leave Bath."

"Yes," Dr. Cooper said, joining the conversation from the other side of the rug. "Father cannot rest while people need assistance. He did his best to retire, due to his own ailments, but when I was overwhelmed with calls, he would assist me anyway."

Evelyn swallowed a smile so she would not appear too much like a cat before cream. Things were going precisely as she had hoped.

"But surely Derham cannot be so busy as to require the both of you," Aunt Edith said.

"I suppose you would be surprised on the number of times my poor brother is called upon in the dead of night," Julia said, accepting a cup of tea and bringing it to her lips.

Father clapped Dr. Cooper on the shoulder. "We are fortunate to have such a competent young man to call on in our times of need."

"Or before we reach desperate need in those early hours of the morning," Evelyn said, gazing into her father's face so he might not misread her meaning. "It is likely better to call on him before we reach such dire straits."

Father held her gaze a moment before chuckling. "But how can one know when one will find themselves in need of a doctor?"

"Many don't know prior to their time of need," Dr. Cooper responded. "Which puts me in mind of Harry. Might I check on the boy?"

"Yes," Evelyn said, rising. She reached forward and set the teapot on the tray, wiping her hands down her skirt.

The occupants in the room all stared at her as though she'd gone mad. Had he meant later?

Dr. Cooper leapt to his feet. "I suppose now is as good a time as any," he said. He shot his sister a look. "Excuse us a moment."

Julia rose as well, setting down her teacup with a hint of sorrow. "I shall accompany you."

They left the library and climbed the stairs toward the twins' chamber. Julia came close behind Evelyn and whispered, "You must tell me the details of your discussion with the duke. I've been dying to hear, and the waiting is pure torment."

"Not now, Julia," Evelyn said in equally hushed tones. They had other things to worry about at present—like the state of Father's health —and besides, she had been grateful for the distraction. "I shall tell you everything later."

Julia glanced over her shoulder toward her brother. Dr. Cooper was not the reason Evelyn intended to wait, but Julia could believe what she wished.

Evelyn reached forward and rapped her knuckles on the door twice before opening it and letting herself into the room. Harry lay in bed, hands resting behind his head as he stared at the ceiling. Jack sat on the bed opposite his brother, reading aloud from a book.

"May we intrude?" Evelyn asked. "Dr. Cooper would like to check your leg, Harry."

Jack closed the book and placed it on the small table beside his bed.

"That would be fine," Harry said, pushing himself to sit up against his headboard. He had done marvelously today sitting still and allowing his leg to heal, but his pure boredom was evident in the draw of his features.

"Perhaps you can show me what you are reading?" Julia asked Jack, coming to sit beside him on the narrow bed. Evelyn crossed the room and stood behind the doctor as he pulled the bandage from Harry's leg and checked the wound. She snuck a glance at the cut on his leg and winced, her dinner swirling in her stomach.

She did not usually have a weak stomach, but the sight of her brother's injury made her ill. If only she had prevented it.

But for Harry, she could be strong. Much as she had the day before when she held his hand while Dr. Cooper worked.

"Your leg looks well, Harry," Dr. Cooper said. "No infection. But watch for redness and swelling, you understand?"

"Yes, Dr. Cooper."

"Very good." Dr. Cooper grinned at the boy before wrapping him back up and gently moving his leg under the blanket once again. "Happy Christmas, young man."

Harry settled back onto his bed, sighing in long-suffering, and they turned to leave. Pausing at the door to wait for Julia, who was listening to Jack tell her something with enthusiasm, Evelyn grasped Dr. Cooper by the hand and pulled him into the corridor.

Wide eyes fell upon her and she whispered urgently, squeezing his fingers. "Something is wrong with my father and he refuses to tell me what it is."

His expression of shock transformed to bewilderment. "What am I meant to do about it?"

"You are a surgeon, Dr. Cooper. Can you not inquire about what ails him?"

"He looks perfectly healthy, Evelyn. What cause do I have to question him?"

She groaned quietly, whispering fiercely. "I gave you a perfectly just cause earlier when I mentioned how he tires in the evenings. You could have used *that*."

"Evelyn," Dr. Cooper said, much as he had when they were children, "most men of your father's age tire easily in the evenings. It is a perfectly acceptable change."

"Very well," she said crisply as she heard the bed shifting inside the room. Julia must be finished. "But promise me you will be mindful of my warnings? I do not wish to be knocking on your door in the middle of the night next."

Dr. Cooper looked appalled. With wild eyes, he shook his head slightly, pulling his hand from her grasp. "Miss Trainor, you must allow me the wisdom and knowledge of my own profession and take me for my word. I shall watch more carefully, but you should watch your tongue."

Her cheeks flushed at once as she recalled the words which had just escaped her lips. Any listening ears would not understand that they'd been previously speaking about the array of townsfolk who knock on Dr. Cooper's door with medical emergencies in the middle of the night.

She had just successfully made herself sound like a trollop.

Turning back toward the room, Evelyn stilled at the sight of her friend standing in the doorway, a displeased expression washing over her face. "Are you ready to return downstairs?" Evelyn asked, though even she could hear how her voice sounded strained.

Lifting her head, Julia nodded. "Of course." She leaned back into the boys' room and said, "Goodnight Jack. Feel better, Harry."

Dr. Cooper was already halfway down the stairs when Evelyn turned back around, and she was grateful for the space. Drawing Julia's arm under her own, Evelyn said, "I just asked your brother to keep a watch on my father, and accidentally made it sound as though I was propositioning him."

"What is new?" Julia asked wryly. "Perhaps you ought to step back and allow your father some privacy."

"Who needs privacy when their very health is in danger?"

"Yes," Julia said quietly, shaking her head, "who indeed?"

They made it to the bottom of the stairs when Julia tugged on Evelyn's arm. Spearing her with a look that was quite solemn, she said, "It is not kind of you to trifle with him."

Evelyn sucked in a quiet, small breath. "What do you mean?"

"My brother. You know he's loved you for some time now. I saw you grasp his hand. But please, do not tug his heart along if you do not return his feelings, Evelyn. I know you to be kinder than that."

A beat of silence passed before Julia released her arm and started toward the library. But Evelyn found she could not move.

It was true; she knew of the doctor's feelings. He had shared them with her himself. But that had been months ago…surely his heart was not still turned toward her.

Guilt filled her body and she squeezed her eyes shut. When had things gone so wrong?

CHAPTER 12

Sanders' drawing room was stuffed with hot air and self-importance.

Mother perched upon the settee opposite Alverton, her mouth outlined in disapproval as she watched him with unabashed interest as he did his best to ignore Miss Rowe.

Mrs. Rowe sat primly on the sofa beside Sanders, her turban covering a mound of badly tinted black hair, and her rouge standing out against pallid skin. And *this* was the refined lineage Alverton was meant to align himself with. His aunt turned to Sanders and began questioning the earl about his sisters' prospects.

"They are quite young, of course. You will not have met them in Society yet," Sanders said.

"I look forward to it," she cooed. "If they are half as well-mannered as you, my lord, then we are sure to absolutely adore them."

Sanders shot Alverton a look above Mrs. Rowe's head. Guilt slithered into Alverton's gut like an unwelcome snake. Whatever could he do to force these women to leave? They were ruining a perfectly good holiday. Perhaps if he suggested an outing…

"Miss Rowe," Alverton said, distancing himself from the young, simpering miss with use of her formal name. "Have you been to see the marvel which is called Stonehenge?"

Widening her eyes, she shook her head. "I have not, your grace. It would be marvelous if we could—"

"It is much too cold and wet for a venture such as that," Mother snapped. "We must remain here until the roads have cleared some and the carriage does not promise to freeze us solid."

"Did you not freeze on your journey to Chesford?" Alverton inquired, tilting his head in feigned innocence.

Mother would have none of that. "Shall we have some music?" she asked instead. "Cassandra has a lovely voice."

Miss Rowe's voice could not be as lovely as Lady Eve's. No, not *Lady Eve*. She was merely Miss Evelyn Trainor.

Alverton's gaze trained on the roaring fire and an equal degree of heat rushed to the back of his neck. He had been mortified when Evelyn disclosed her secret. Utterly and supremely mortified. What had she thought? That by snagging his attention as a lady, he would be inclined to look past the inferiority of her birth *and* her dishonesty? It did not matter what she had said in her own defense. She'd lied about her own name. How was he to know what else she'd lied about?

Perhaps she'd meant for the facade to carry on forever.

Well, she needn't have. She'd have only needed the facade to hold up until the wedding vows were exchanged.

"Your grace, I should very much like to sing for you if you wish."

Alverton looked up to find Miss Rowe standing directly in front of him. Her flawless, pale complexion was only ruined by the use of rouge upon her cheeks, just like her mother's, and her light blue eyes were clear, her blonde curls brought back and arranged just so. She was the perfect candidate for a duchess. His mother was right. She had the decorum and the grace to appear the duchess, and the training to withstand the rigors which came along with the duty.

But Miss Rowe was not *her*. Miss Rowe was not the woman he imagined spending his days with. She was not the woman he had thought about incessantly over the last week. He would never marry

Evelyn Trainor. He could not. But the woman he had begun to fall for, the imaginary Lady Eve, he still held onto the idea of *that* woman.

There was no way around it. Lady Eve had set the standard by which he would judge every woman hereafter. Which was such a shame, really.

Because Lady Eve did not exist.

"You may play," Alverton said with a flick of his wrist. The coy smile Miss Rowe delivered was both nauseating and obnoxious. He turned on his seat to face Sanders, who had patience sufficient to manage ridiculous young ladies. Perhaps if Alverton had younger sisters, he too would remain calm and unbothered.

Miss Rowe began warming her fingers up on the pianoforte on the far side of the room, sending her cat-like smile Alverton's way periodically. He could sense her predatory nature and the way she viewed him as prey. But he would not succumb to her artful tactics.

"Perhaps we ought to prepare to return to London, Sanders," Alverton said, inspecting the cuff of his sleeve.

A harsh chord sounded on the pianoforte and he glanced up to find Miss Rowe's wide, panicked eyes on him.

"A fortnight earlier than planned?" Sanders asked, his eyebrow raised.

Alverton shrugged, ignoring his young cousin as she began to play. "I have found that all which initially drew me here has flagged and nothing could possibly keep me here any longer."

"Nothing?"

Alverton read the meaning in his friend's tone. He was likely referring to Evelyn, as he had made comments regarding her since their initial meeting in the lane. Sanders himself had found unlikely friends in her young brothers. But Alverton did not blame him for that; there was something about Harry and Jack which reminded him of himself and Sanders at that same age when they had met at school.

"I am at your leisure," Sanders said. But in truth, the reverse was true. It was Sanders' holiday which Alverton had joined, and Sanders' holiday which would be cut horribly short because of Alverton's female relations.

Miss Rowe began to sing along with her playing and Alverton clenched his teeth. Her voice was not bad. In fact, had he not had Evelyn's voice in his mind, he would believe Miss Rowe to be prodigious talented, indeed.

But that was the rub. He could not remove from his mind a very delicate alto which haunted his dreams and played in his mind during the day.

Overcome with frustration, Alverton did what he could to remain seated for the duration of Miss Rowe's performance. It was not her fault—however obnoxious she was—that Evelyn had ruined him for all other voices. His body hummed with energy and his limbs ached to be held so still.

At the completion of her performance, Alverton rose, clapping his hands in conjunction with the other occupants in the room. Miss Rowe stood, delivering a curtsy and a satisfied smile.

"You must excuse me," Alverton said, offering no further explanation. He dipped his torso in a bow and turned, fleeing the room at once.

Sanders' voice could be heard as he left the room. He did not know what the man was saying, but he hoped it was an excuse to follow him.

He could use a friend right now.

Letting himself into Sanders' study, Alverton paced the room from the hearth to the window. He waited a quarter of an hour with no interruptions before he pulled the bell with more force than necessary. Standing in the center of the room, staring at the study door, he waited.

A young maid opened the door and jumped when her eyes landed on the duke, still as a statue and watching the door, his hands grasped behind his back.

"I need Sanders," he said briskly.

She dipped a curtsy and hurried from the room.

Alverton resumed his pacing, turning again when the door opened. But it was not Sanders.

It was Miss Rowe.

"Perhaps I can be of assistance," she said meekly, stepping inside and closing the door softly behind herself.

Alverton knew her meekness to be a game.

"It appears my mother did not pass along the message," Alverton said, at ease. It was perhaps the first time since that dreadful moment with Evelyn in the grove that he felt relaxed. But he *had* warned Mother that he wouldn't abide any more compromising attempts from Miss Rowe, so he need not fear repercussions for what he was about to say.

"What message is that, your grace?" Miss Rowe asked, stepping closer.

He remained where he was on the center of the rug, though he longed to approach the girl and use his height to intimidate her. "That I will not be compromised. If you wish that path for yourself, then you will suffer the consequences. Alone."

She seemed to grow still, her eyes unblinking, searching his gaze as though debating the validity of his claim. "I don't know what you mean, your grace."

"Precisely what I said. You may do what you wish to attempt to secure my title, but I will not marry you. So you must do so with the knowledge that you are only ruining yourself."

She dropped her facade, facing him with a look that spoke of more intelligence than he realized she possessed. Her voice was low, a hard edge coloring her tone. "I have a hard time believing, your grace, that you would allow your own family's name to be dragged through the mud. To speak nothing of the *Alverton* name and the scandal which would undoubtedly attach itself to you were such a thing to occur. I cannot think the *ton* would take kindly to a duke who allowed a proper young woman to become compromised and left her to be ruined. Your father never would have stood for it."

He nearly stepped backward from the blow. She was correct; Father never would have stood for it. The ultimate example of doing his duty to the title and his family, Father would have commanded the union after Miss Rowe's first attempts to compromise him.

Alverton was not his father, however. He could do his best to live up to the prestige and honesty his father had hammered into him from his youth, but he did not have to marry a slithering, deceitful young woman simply because she knew where his weakness lay.

"What you are not taking into account," Alverton replied acidly, straightening his shoulders, "is that I am the duke and you are a miss. I can get away with nearly whatever I wish, and the *ton* will look away. You, however, cannot."

She glared at him with the heat of a Yule log and he stared directly back with cool reserve. Contentedness settled upon his shoulders. He could still be the man his father raised him to be without settling for a wife he cared little for.

It was this scene which Sanders opened the door and discovered, his shocked eyebrows rising high on his forehead.

"Excuse me," Miss Rowe said, slipping past the earl. She cast Alverton a final look and he very much thought she infused it with the words, *this is not over yet, your grace.*

Sanders closed the door securely behind himself before crossing the carpet and falling into a plump burgundy chair. "What is it, Alverton? You seem to be a wreck."

Alverton scrubbed a hand over his face before joining his friend. He let his head fall back on the chair, gazing at the wood-paneled ceiling and tracing the panels one by one with his eyes. "The girl refuses to accept that *I* cannot be compromised, but *she* can."

"Do you mean to imply that I stepped into another attempt?"

"Yes."

Sanders cursed. "Your own mother brought her here."

"And I did warn my mother of my resolve, but the woman is determined. She is so caught up in needing to see me wed that she cares not the path which will take me to the alter. Nor the girl, it would seem. It is as though she has determined my marriage status to be her only objective since my father died."

Sanders chuckled. "You paint a very bleak picture of your mother."

"My mother has painted the picture herself. I informed her that if Miss Rowe proceeds to act this way she will only ruin herself and I shall not save her name."

Sanders looked pained. "This was not how this holiday was meant to go."

"And for that I must apologize."

"It is not your fault, Alverton," Sanders said compassionately. "You could not have known they would follow you here."

Alverton turned wry eyes on his friend. "You are a good man, Sanders. Perhaps I shall buy you a horse when all this is through to thank you for your troubles."

"I shall attend Tattersall's with you and choose the very finest."

Alverton chuckled, facing the fire. He watched the flames flicker, licking the hearth. Scent of the evergreen boughs trimming the mantle tickled his nose and he sighed. It was proving to be a very sorry Christmas, thus far.

"But your family is not the only reason you have been sour, is it?" Sanders asked.

It was almost as though the man could read minds. Not two beats of the clock after Alverton began to picture Evelyn in his mind, wondering how she spent her holiday, the earl brought up the root of Alverton's disquiet.

"Did something occur?"

"Yes."

Sanders waited a moment before asking, "And do you wish to tell me what it was?"

"Lady Eve."

"A woman," he said, his voice dry. "And here I thought we'd come to Chesford to escape women. It appears we do not have that choice."

"Did you ever notice that no one in the house referred to either of the boys as lords?"

"Yes," Sanders said slowly. "But they are children. It is not so very odd to leave off the courtesy title."

Alverton sat up, holding his friend's gaze. "It is not because they are children, or even due to the trauma of the injury. It was because they are not lords. Lady Eve is not a lady. She is Miss Evelyn Trainor."

Understanding lit Sanders' eyes. "I *thought* I recognized her. We played as children a time or two. Never so much as to know her on sight, but evidently enough to jog my memory. Who is her father?"

"Mr. Trainor, of the House of Commons."

Sanders nodded again, knowingly. "I should have made the connection on my own. But we never come to Chesford and I hardly know most of the people here."

"I do not blame you," Alverton said at once.

Sanders leaned back in his seat, running a hand through his hair. "And yet, this could have been avoided."

Shaking his head, Alverton sighed. "I feel ill-used. I could not tell she was a title-hunter on the onset. But that is not the worst of it."

"Oh?"

"No," Alverton continued. "The worst of it is that regardless of how angry I am, I cannot quit thinking about her."

CHAPTER 13

After spending the entire morning reading to a poor, bedridden Harry, Evelyn required some sunlight and fresh air. She tied her bonnet under her chin, pulling her cape tightly around her neck.

"Where are you off to?" Aunt Edith inquired from the parlor, drawing Evelyn's attention. Crossing the hall, Evelyn hovered in the doorway. Her aunt waited for an answer, displeasure evident in her expression; or perhaps that was simply how she always felt. It was certainly how she usually looked.

"To visit with Julia," Evelyn said. "I would like to purchase red thread for my sampler, and I planned to ask if she would accompany me."

Aunt Edith watched her, the older woman's mouth pinched. "You have let a good opportunity pass you by this last fortnight," she said, surprising Evelyn.

Evelyn pressed a hand to her stomach. "I cannot think what you mean."

"There is an earl and a duke residing just across the grove and you've done nothing to attempt to secure either man."

Evelyn scoffed. "Have we not discussed this? I am not eligible for either title. Father's lack of fortune aside, our name is not elevated enough for such a match."

"It is not so absurd, Evelyn," she bit back. "You are a gentleman's daughter. You do your brothers and myself a disservice with your lack of effort."

"Whatever do my brothers have to do with who I marry?" Furthermore, how would her choice in husband effect Aunt Edith?

"They are young, yet. Do you want to see them go to the poorhouse?"

Her blood rushed down to her feet, and Evelyn felt her head grow dizzy. "Please explain yourself," she whispered.

Aunt Edith held her gaze. "Funds diminish. And nothing is being done to replenish them. Your father was counting on you to make a good match this Season which might support us all. But you have been too selfish by half, caring more for the museums and the park than the balls and the gentlemen. You would rather us all rot than accept a gentleman's courtship."

Cool ice slithered down her spine. "I did not know," Evelyn said. "You did not tell me."

"Your father forbade it. He wanted me to spare you the concern." Aunt Edith closed her eyes, leaning her head back against the chair. "But now look at the position we are in. A few more months, perhaps, and we are *all* off to the poorhouse."

Evelyn swallowed, fear and anxiety filling her person like a thousand tiny bugs. She had heard stories of the men and women forced to go to the poorhouse. Her brothers could never survive such a horrid place, to say nothing of her father, or her aunt.

She, of course, would sacrifice anything for their wellbeing. Turning from her aunt, she fled the house, walking briskly toward Derham as though her quick steps could carry her from the troubles spat at her by her aunt.

If only they had kept her apprised of the situation. If only her aunt had explained before they set off for London that she had it within her power to save them, that they *needed* saving. Then Evelyn might have put in some effort.

Humiliation and shame overcame her and she paused at the tree halfway through the grove. Gentlemen had shown her interest before, and she had merely put them off. One man in particular had expressed his interest in her on more than one occasion, but as the feelings were not returned, Evelyn had merely done her best to forget them.

Determination slowly formed in her chest and spread outward. It was not too late. And this particular man's feelings were likely somewhat the same. The last time he had inquired about the state of her heart was just before she left for the London Season, and she had politely turned him down. Leaning against the tree's thick, wide trunk, she made a promise to herself.

She would do whatever she must to help her family. Even if it meant marrying a man she didn't love.

Pushing away from the tree, determined, Evelyn made her way toward Derham and the Cooper's house. She had a very important call to make.

❊

Dr. Cooper was away from home, and Evelyn could not help but feel grateful that her uncomfortable call could be put off.

Julia had agreed to an outing and outfitted herself in a pelisse and bonnet, joining Evelyn by the arm and walking down the street toward the shop. It was not snowing presently, but the ground remained frozen and mud was forming alongside the cobblestone road.

"Have you heard of the ball on Twelfth Night?" Julia asked. "I cannot decide whether to wear my jonquil gown, or the one made of red crepe."

"I should think the jonquil will set off your hair to perfection. And the delicate embroidery is nothing to smirk at."

Julia grinned. "Yes, it does make my eyes look fine, does it not?"

"And is there a certain gentleman you are hoping to look fine for?" Evelyn asked, half-jesting.

Julia's silence was telling and Evelyn could not help but pause in the street and turn toward her friend. They did not keep secrets from one another. "What is it you are not telling me?"

Julia sucked in a breath, her mouth looking as though it wanted to smile but she was not allowing it the privilege. "I am afraid to speak the words aloud," she whispered.

Evelyn reached forward to squeeze her friend's hand, attempting to portray her support. "I care for you, Julia. I shall not do or say anything which might jeopardize our friendship. You may trust me if you wish to. But if you would rather not say, I shall respect that as well."

Carriage wheels sounded on the cobblestones behind them and Evelyn guided Julia away from the street, stepping over a patch of mud.

Glancing over her shoulder, Evelyn froze. The carriage was very fine with a crest emblazoned on the side in red and gold. She was not a simpleton. This could only belong to one man: Alverton.

She searched the windows as they rumbled past, against her better judgement, but was unable to see past the woman who sat on the edge —an older woman with gray hair pulled up into a cap and a displeased expression on her mouth.

"Do you think they are leaving Derham?" Julia asked, clearly having deduced the inhabitants of the carriage as well.

"I wouldn't know."

The horses pulled up the road and came to a slow stop before a footman hopped from the back and came around to open the door and let down the step. Evelyn and Julia watched, transfixed as three well-dressed women were let out of the carriage, followed by a single man.

Evelyn's breath caught in her chest when polished Hessian boots stepped from the carriage, but she was immediately disappointed to see the lighter brown hair belonging to Lord Sanders peeking from under his hat.

Hope pulsed within her until the footman closed the door and put up the step.

Alverton had not joined them.

Sighing, Evelyn turned to her friend. "Shall we quit watching them as though they are tigers in a menagerie? I am still in need of red thread."

Julia took her by the arm and led her toward the shop. It did not escape her notice that the party had entered the same shop and Evelyn told herself it did not matter. Lord Sanders had likely been informed of her deceit and would give her the cut direct—which she most definitely deserved. Swallowing the bitter taste in her mouth, Evelyn stepped inside the shop.

If only she had been honest from the beginning.

"Such a quaint little town," a young woman was saying. "Such cute little houses. However do you think people live inside them? All pushed together as they are, I mean. There cannot be room to turn around."

Julia froze beside Evelyn and she took her friend's arm for support. If things went the way Evelyn planned, she could very well be residing in one of those houses herself. And there was certainly nothing wrong with that scenario.

"They are poor, Cassandra," an older woman said. "They do not know any better."

A third woman, regal and prim, spoke to the shop girl. "Have you any fans?"

"Yes, madam. Allow me a moment to fetch them."

Lord Sanders stepped away from the party, grazing the items along the wall slowly. He turned, pausing when he caught sight of the women standing near the door. Evelyn held his gaze a moment before casting her gaze to the wooden floor, ashamed anew by the knowing light in his eyes.

He approached, his boots causing a loud, jarring echo in the room. Dipping a bow, he said, "Miss Trainor."

Evelyn's face flushed and she turned, catching his pale blue gaze. What did he wish to say to her? She swallowed her apprehension when his eyes flicked toward Julia. "Lord Sanders," she said, finding her voice and dipping a curtsy, "allow me to introduce my friend, Miss Cooper."

"The doctor's sister?" Lord Sanders asked.

"Yes, my lord," Julia said. "Are you acquainted with my brother?"

"Indeed. Very good man."

"He is," she agreed. They looked at one another a moment longer before Lord Sanders turned his attention to Evelyn.

"Did you enjoy your Christmas?"

Despite facing disappointment from multiple areas, she had enjoyed Christmas day. The quaintly decorated rooms with evergreen boughs and holly, and gathering with loved ones around the Yule log had warmed her soul in a much needed way. She nodded.

"And do you plan to attend the Twelfth Night assemblies in town?" he asked, turning to Julia to include her in the question.

"I do not—"

Julia cut her off. "Yes. We do. We both shall be attending the assemblies."

"Very good. I look forward to seeing you there. Perhaps," Lord Sanders paused, looking over his shoulder at the women standing before the counter. The youngest of his guests watched with interest, her fair complexion wrinkled in confusion. He settled back on Julia. "Miss Cooper, might I have the first set?"

Her cheeks grew pink, but Julia held his gaze. "Of course, my lord."

"And Miss Trainor," he said, turning toward Evelyn. "Might I claim the second?"

Shock bloomed in her chest. He knew of her deceit, for he had called her properly by her own name. And still he wished to dance with her? Alverton could not have forgiven her so readily, of course. But why had Lord Sanders?

Silence stretched a moment too long, perhaps, for Julia's foot reached under Evelyn's gown and kicked her softly on the boot. "Yes, my lord," Evelyn said quickly. "I would be honored."

He bowed again. "Until the ball."

The women curtsied to Lord Sanders, keeping quiet as he gathered his guests and escorted them outside the shop.

"What in heaven's name was that about?" Julia asked quietly, watching the earl through the window.

"I haven't the faintest," Evelyn responded. "But he certainly knows all, or he would not have called me by the correct name."

"If only I had the wherewithal to ask if the duke would be attending," Julia said. "But I could not think straight with his striking eyes trained on me just so. They were the exact color of a winter sky."

Evelyn could not help but grin. "Julia, you shock me. What shall you do when you dance with him if you cannot make conversation in a shop?"

"I shall hope we are dancing very involved reels, and that I am not called upon for conversation. For I do not know what I will say."

The women laughed together, but Evelyn could not remove from her mind the interested gaze of the younger woman. She was not jealous, as a suitor of Lord Sanders would have been by his requesting the first two sets of dances. And that, in Evelyn's mind, could only mean one thing.

The young woman was after the duke, instead.

CHAPTER 14

*H*iding behind a tree like a small child was well beneath Alverton's rank and age, but he could not help it. When he'd heard the quick footsteps originally, he'd intended to stand his ground, allow the woman to pass him, and deliver the cut direct like any foibled Peer ought to do in his situation.

But then Evelyn had come into view, so utterly distraught, and he'd lost his resolve.

Instead of teaching her a well-deserved lesson, Alverton had jumped behind a cluster of trees and peeked through their branches, utterly hidden from view and able to watch Evelyn lean against the massive tree, dropping her head in her hands and expelling shuddering breaths.

Oh, how he longed to cross the distance and pull her into his arms. To stroke her silky hair and whisper to her that he could make her troubles cease.

She had been ruthlessly dishonest, and he found he could not forgive her lies. But that did not discount the troubles she faced regarding her father's health or her brothers' well-being.

If only he could be assured that those were the only troubles she faced. Alas, there was no way to ascertain without approaching her. And that was simply something he could not do.

But he could watch her now without anyone the wiser, and he allowed himself to soak in her beauty for one more moment.

And then she looked up. Alverton paused, for she was looking nearly directly at him and he wondered if she could see him through the trees. Her face had gone from distressed to resolved, and he could see in her mannerisms that she had come to a decision of some sort.

And blast his rebellious heart, he passionately wished to know the nature of that resolve.

Instead, he held his breath, and his tongue, while Evelyn continued on the path through the grove, passing by his tree just an arm's length away.

When the sound of her soft footsteps against the frozen ground dissipated, Alverton sighed, leaning his forehead against the tree. It was cold, and he only remained that way a moment before turning onto the path.

If Evelyn was gone, then he could slip through the grove and to the Trainor's house quickly to check on young Harry. The idea grew more pleasant as he considered the various components of his scheme and he was already walking toward the house before he'd determined that it was a safe option.

A tall, stately butler answered the door and admitted him into the foyer at once. "The master is in the library, your grace."

The object of his visit vanished immediately as this fortunate happenstance was brought to light and Alverton nodded, following the butler toward the library. Curiosity coursed through him. He was not going to miss the opportunity to meet Evelyn's father.

The last time he'd entered that particular room he'd been carrying a young, injured boy. In the light of day, the library had a much less ominous feel to it.

But he would refrain from sitting on the leather sofa, all the same.

"Mr. Trainor," Alverton said, dipping his head.

Using his cane, Mr. Trainor pushed himself to his feet at once, bowing to the duke. "What do I owe this pleasure, your grace?" the man asked, his mustache quivering.

"Forgive me, but I've come to call on young master Harry."

The older man's eyebrows hitched up. "Send for him," he said over the duke's shoulder, likely to the butler, and Alverton lifted a hand at once.

"He needn't be bothered. I can go to him."

"Nonsense. The boy has been rearing to leave his bedchamber and this is a good enough excuse."

Alverton's mouth slipped into a small smile. He was glad to be considered *good enough* by Mr. Trainor.

"I know you are a Tory, your grace, and I shall do my best not to hold it against you," Mr. Trainor said, gesturing to the leather chair near his own.

Alverton could not help but chuckle at the man's wit, as he lowered himself into the seat. The man had gumption to address a duke in such a comfortable manner, so Alverton delivered equal frankness. "And I heard that you ought to retire, and yet you stubbornly refuse."

Mr. Trainor tilted his head, his eyes narrowing. "You've been talking to my daughter, I presume?"

"Some," Alverton admitted.

"Bah. Poppycock, that's what I say."

"You needn't step down for the good of your health?"

Mr. Trainor stared at the duke unapologetically. "I need to *remain* for the good of my health. Are you married, your grace?"

"No," Alverton answered, surprised by the turn of conversation. He began to harden his resolve, prepared to flee at a moment's notice. Was this man following his daughter's plan, or perhaps the other way around?

"Then you may not understand this. But my wife died in childbirth, delivering my sons nearly ten years ago. Ten years, young man. Do you realize how very long that is?"

"I can imagine," he replied. This was certainly not the direction he'd anticipated this conversation going, and it had been quite a long time since he'd been referred to as a young man. He rather appreciated Mr. Trainor's gall.

Mr. Trainor sighed. "I loved my wife dearly, you see. And while I have much to be grateful for, I cannot be *here* in this house and not miss her. I miss her so deeply that it pains me, and it is not a pain which my beautiful daughter or my lively sons can fix. They are not my beloved wife."

"And so you devote yourself to politics," Alverton finished, understanding settling on his shoulders.

Mr. Trainor nodded. He leaned back in his seat, closing his eyes.

"You know," he said with familiarity, "I have always enjoyed your speeches, your grace. You are quite brilliant for a Tory."

Alverton smiled, his body relaxing into his own chair. Footsteps sounded in the corridor outside the library and the door squeaked open, admitting a footman carrying a young boy, another boy trailing close behind them.

"How is our young pirate-hunter today?" Alverton asked.

"Bored," Harry answered. The footman set him on the sofa and he sat up, stretching his legs across the length of the cushions. Jack sat on the other end of the couch, watching the duke with wide-eyed reverence.

"Has the doctor returned to check your leg?" Alverton asked. Soft snoring to his left grabbed his attention and he turned to find Mr. Trainor soundly asleep.

"I'm healing along fine," Harry said. "But he doesn't want me walking until tomorrow."

Alverton raised his eyebrow. "You will be careful, I presume?"

Harry nodded rapidly. "Evelyn won't let me outside if I'm not."

Alverton's heart constricted at the familiar use of her name. He longed to inquire after her, but worried about the forwardness of such a thing. Shooting a glance to the older man, he confirmed Mr. Trainor's sleep before asking, "And is she here?"

"No," Jack said. "She's gone off to town."

"London?" he asked, though he knew it was not true. He simply wanted to hear more about her errand.

Jack laughed. "Derham. I heard Aunt Edith tell her to find a husband there."

Alverton paused. That made very little sense. "How is she to manage that?"

Jack lifted a shoulder. "I don't know. But I know it's important."

"Oh?" Alverton did his best to sound uninterested. It was a feat, indeed, for the information he was receiving was very, *very* interesting.

Jack nodded, swallowing. "She must, if she is going to save us from the poorhouse."

Alverton stilled. He would not ask the boy to repeat his words for there was no way he had misheard him, however much he wished to. But if Mr. Trainor was in such dire straits, would he not do something himself to save his family?

No, he would not. Where would the sense be in such a thing when he had a perfectly beautiful daughter, poised and elegant, with a natural talent to sing and win men's hearts available? He could much more easily marry her off and receive the security he needed that way.

Bile rose in his throat and Alverton stood quickly. It was all too much. Coming here had been a mistake.

Alverton smiled at the red-headed boy. "I hope you can return to your ship tomorrow, Harry. But be careful or you will ruin your leg forever."

"You sound like my sister," Harry said.

Alverton did not know whether that was a compliment or not, but judging by the distaste on the boy's face, it certainly was not meant as one.

"Good day, boys."

They said farewell and Alverton let himself out. Crossing the snowy lawn, he picked his way through the grove and marched to Chesford Place.

He could not allow himself to pity Evelyn's plight, for it was likely that horrible circumstance which forced her into her deceitful actions.

But all the same, he did not rejoice in her trials, either.

Letting himself into Chesford, he slammed the door too loudly, the sound reverberating from the empty foyer's walls. Silence met him and he was glad he had not agreed to go into Derham with the ladies. He needed the silence and peace to consider the new information and how he would process it.

For Evelyn needed to marry a man of means, and that man could not be him.

CHAPTER 15

It had been days since Evelyn had seen the duke, but that did not stop her from thinking about him. Her traitorous heart did little else.

And yet, she needed to find a way. It was inevitable; she needed to wed. She had a man chosen particularly for the very purpose whom she was nearly certain would accept her proposal.

The difficulty lay in completing the task. Each time Evelyn convinced herself to return to town and seek out Dr. Cooper, she balked. He was a good man and he would make a comfortable, fair husband. But he did not have her heart.

Evelyn descended the stairs. If only she could locate her brothers, then she could use them to distract herself.

A knock came at the front door and the butler appeared out of nowhere, opening it and ushering a woman inside, snow and wind sneaking into the house with her.

"Julia?" Evelyn asked, recognizing the cloak shrouding her friend.

Julia's face was concerned, and Evelyn flew down the stairs with haste.

"What is it?" she asked, resting her hands upon her friend's forearms.

"We've received word that there is a family in the church with nothing." Julia was breathless, shadows falling over her face in the dim corridor. Evelyn debated whether she should guide her friend to a seat or remain standing when Julia continued. "They traveled to Derham on the hope that their family would take them in but came to discover that their family is long gone."

"Who is it?"

"The Jacobsens," Julia said.

"But they left for London over a year ago," Evelyn said. "Julia, can I get you some tea? Won't you come sit down a moment?"

The woman's breaths heaved as though she'd run all the way from the center of town. Snow clung to her shoulders and glittered from her bonnet.

She shook her head. "I cannot. I've only come to inquire what sort of assistance you might offer. They are quite willing to serve and the oldest daughter worked as an undermaid in an estate up north before a fire swept the land and they lost everything, including her position."

Evelyn sucked in a breath. "How horrible."

Julia paused and Evelyn realized, belatedly, that it was time for her to offer assistance. But what could she do? They were not in a position to take in an entire family. "We do not have need of additional servants. Indeed, we do not have the space or the requirement."

"Mr. Hart has agreed to house them in the rectory until a permanent situation can be found, but the mother is with child and in dire straits. Mr. Hart is not equipped to care for her." Shaking her head in wonder, Julia said, "I'm not sure how they even traveled all this way in such conditions."

"What of the Hollingsfords?" Evelyn asked. She did not hold a strong acquaintance with the family, but surely with their affluence they would be in a position to help. "Do they have a cottage available on their land?"

Julia's eyes hardened. "Jared went to them and they refused. He would not divulge the particulars to me, but suffice it to say this sort of charity is beneath them."

"How they will be comfortable sitting in church with that sort of opinion goes beyond my comprehension," Evelyn said. "Very well. I shall do what I can. Allow me to find my father and I shall contrive a plan. Where might I find you?"

"The vicarage."

Julia's shoes clicked away and Evelyn waited for the front door to close before she sank onto a spindle back chair against the wall and leaned her elbow on a decorative table. Her mind worked around the problem until she determined to approach her father and ask his opinion. He was resourceful, after all, and would do what he could to help the family, surely.

Even if they did not have funds to hire the family as servants, surely their charity could extend to assisting them until they developed a more permanent plan.

She approached the library, opening the door and stepping inside. "Father, there is trouble at the vicarage and I am afraid I cannot conceive of an appropriate—"

She halted on the rug as she came around the chairs and her eyes caught the familiar dark gaze of the duke.

Alverton.

But what was he doing in her library? And with her father, no less.

"What is it, dear?" Father asked, his white eyebrows drawn together in concern, completely unaware of the underlying currents traveling between Alverton and Evelyn.

Evelyn's throat had gone dry. She tried to swallow but her throat felt much like sand. Pulling her gaze away from Alverton's serious, brown eyes and training it on her father, she said, "A family has arrived in town with nothing and nowhere to go. Mr. Hart is keeping them until they can find a permanent solution. It seems they've come anticipating the Jacobsens' welcome and did not realize that the family had moved away."

"The Jacobsens left quite some time ago," Father said. "And I do not know how we can be of any help now. Have you spoken to Mrs. Bosch?"

The housekeeper? "No," Evelyn said. "I came straight to you,

Father. The mother is in a delicate condition and it would behoove us, I think, to find a way to assist them."

Father turned to Alverton, a boyish grin developing on his face. "Is this not what we were just discussing, your grace? It is my duty as a member of this parish to assist those within my boundaries who require help."

"Yes, but this family hardly counts. They only just arrived." His low voice sent a shiver down Evelyn's spine. She had missed the sound of his voice the last few days and it was all she could do to remain composed. But then he turned his serious gaze on her and a blush rushed to her cheeks. Alverton continued, "You have no way to verify the truth of their claims. How can you be certain they are not simply taking advantage of you?"

His underlying meaning cut through her and she wanted to run from the room. Lifting her chin, she remained, her gaze refusing to leave the duke's.

"Should that matter?" Father said. "If we make the choice to help, then we shall walk away with integrity, regardless of their choices. *They* are the ones, if indeed they are being dishonest, who shall have to live with themselves."

Evelyn could see the men falling back into conversation and found the opportunity to escape. It would be pointless to attempt to accomplish anything now. Father was right; she ought to discuss the issue with their housekeeper. She turned away, making it to the door before her name was called, effectively stopping her.

"Miss Trainor."

She turned to find Alverton standing beside the chair he'd previously been occupying, his gaze fixed on her.

"Yes, your grace?"

He cleared his throat, his gaze darting to her father then landing back on her. "Might I request your presence for a walk in the garden?"

How did one respectfully deny a duke? She glanced to the window and the cold, icy world beyond. He must have required privacy if he was willing to endure a walk in the frigid garden.

"I planned to walk to Derham, your grace. But I must speak to my housekeeper first. I can meet you in the garden in a quarter of an hour, if you'd like to escort me as far as the road."

He nodded once succinctly and then lowered himself in his chair once more. And Evelyn escaped.

Finding her cape and bonnet, she tied both of them securely before snatching her gloves from the table in her chamber and descending the stairs slowly. She found Mrs. Bosch and together determined that they could take on two servants for a short time while the family found a more permanent situation.

Moving toward the front foyer, anticipation caused her hands to shake as she pulled her gloves on one finger at a time. She approached the door and waited.

What was she thinking? She should not have accepted Alverton's escort. His biting looks and angry words would do nothing to assist her at this time. She should go now, before he was able to escape Father's political diatribe.

Evelyn unlatched the door and the wind pushed it open and slammed it against the wall, wet snow diving indoors and chilling her at once.

"Leaving already?" a deep voice said behind her.

She squeezed her eyes shut before looking over her shoulder and finding Alverton's gaze aimed at her. "Now I am, your grace."

She stepped outside, Alverton following close behind her, into the harsh weather. He pulled the door closed, gripping his coat in his hands to close it tighter around his neck.

Clasping her hands firmly behind her back, Evelyn stepped away from the duke, allowing an appropriate amount of distance between them. She would do whatever she could to avoid having Alverton think she was vying for his attention.

Of course, he was the one who came to her house.

"I am surprised you are still here, your grace."

He kept his hands clasped behind his back as he walked beside her. Their progression was slow through the open valley as wind and snow blew against them.

"I could not leave Sanders to entertain my family alone."

"And you chose not to escort your family to London instead and leave Lord Sanders in peace?"

He paused, forcing Evelyn to stop and look over her shoulder at him.

"In truth, I had not thought of that option." A small smile graced his lips and he probably chuckled, but the sound was lost in the wind.

He said something, his voice low, but she could not understand him.

"I apologize, your grace," Evelyn all but shouted, stepping nearer, "but I cannot hear in this wind."

His eyebrows pulled together, his head bending to look into her eyes. She was close enough to him now that the wind was largely blocked by his body and the sweet reprieve caused her heart to flutter.

She could not deny it; she had feelings for the duke.

"Come," he said loudly, his hand slipping over hers. He pulled her toward the game trail in Sanders Grove and the moment they stepped within the woods the wind quieted, the harsh weather subdued.

Evelyn's nerves raced. Alverton's hand still held hers securely, and she did her best not to assume he meant more by it than assisting her from the snow.

"Much better," he said. His gaze darted around the trees, pulling her further into the woods and away from the oncoming storm. They paused in the center of the grove near the large oak tree and Alverton halted, releasing her hand.

She felt instantly bereft.

The man was tall and his attitude imposing. At times she wondered at the audacity of his own self-importance, but clearly he had been raised to value his rank and esteem himself above those of lesser birth. She could not blame him for that which his parents had taught him to believe. And though she had grown to care for him—for underneath his judgmental exterior she was sure by his subtle kindnesses to her brothers and his own friend that a warm heart resided within him—she could not force him to forget a lifetime of consequence for her.

"You should return home," he said.

"I cannot. I am expected at the vicarage and I will not let them down." The wind howled around them as the storm worsened even as they stood within the sanctuary of the grove. Snowflakes darted past the barren branches and fell lazily around them as they stood facing one another, both of their shoulders set stubbornly.

"Your father can complete the errand just as efficiently."

Had he not just sat with her father in the library? The man struggled to walk due to his own weakness and constantly fell asleep. Of course he could not complete the errand just as efficiently. "I must disagree with you."

Alverton shook his head. "I have visited with your father numerous times the last few days and learned of his determination. He will achieve whatever he wishes to."

He'd been visiting with her father regularly? "For what purpose?"

A small smile fell upon Alverton's mouth and Evelyn found she could not look away as he spoke. "We've discussed politics, mostly. He's not all bad, for a Whig."

She could tell the words were spoken kindly, and her heart bloomed in response. The wind whipped around them and Evelyn tore her gaze from the duke's lips. "I must go. You must allow me to make my own decisions, your grace. I am perfectly capable of finding my way to the vicarage."

He stared at her, bothered, no doubt, by her refusal to accept him at his word. "Then I must accompany you."

She lifted her chin. "You will do no such thing."

"I cannot allow you to go alone."

"And I cannot abide your company, your grace."

He stepped back suddenly as though her words had been an assault on his person. Hurt momentarily splashed across his face and Evelyn immediately regretted the harshness of her words. But she'd meant them. Alverton was a constant reminder of her own deceit.

"Forgive me," he said coldly. "I did not realize that my presence was such a hardship."

"How could you not?" she said, surprised at her own boldness. "I cannot even *think* of you without shame overcoming me. I cannot stand to see you, for I am reminded of my own glaring faults."

She'd shocked him. His mouth hung slack while his gaze raked over her. Did he imagine he was the only one suffering for her lies?

"I must go," she said softly. "I need to deliver my message and return before this storm forces me to stay in Derham."

"No," he said, lifting his hand. "It is not safe. If you will not allow my escort, then at least permit me to send a servant on your behalf. The vicar will understand, given the circumstances."

Wind howled around them like a wolf as though it was on the duke's side. Evelyn drew in a breath, painfully keeping Alverton's gaze. She felt a string connecting them, drawing her closer to him. Did he feel a similar connection?

He stepped closer, dipping his head to better look into her eyes. "I will take your silence as acceptance, Miss Trainor. What would you like the note to say?"

She swallowed, finding it uneasy to breathe regularly. "We can create space for two temporary servants, but we are unable to commit to any permanent positions at this time. They may arrive at their earliest convenience. I had the thought—"

She paused. This was her own conjecture, not for the note. But the duke didn't need to hear it.

"Tell me," he prompted.

She looked up; his face was calm, and his eyes were kind. It was the expression she was used to seeing before her lies had been made known and it warmed her soul immensely.

"Please?" he asked.

"It is nothing," she said. "I merely wondered if the mother should go stay with the Coopers. Dr. Cooper would never turn away a woman in need, particularly when her need is of the medical variety. And Julia would take good care of the woman. At least until the storm passes, or they find a home."

"The Coopers are unparalleled, are they not?" he asked, his voice dry.

"They are good people, if that is what you mean."

"Are you planning to marry the doctor?" he asked, suddenly, stepping closer.

Evelyn sucked in a breath, heart hammering at his nearness. How could he know such a thing? She had not even told Dr. Cooper of her scheme, so new and fresh it was in her mind.

"You are, aren't you?" he said, his eyes gleaming with curiosity.

She continued to keep her mouth closed. Silent against his anxious face, she could sense her own breath increasing in speed as the duke drew closer to her. And yet, she could not bring herself to speak.

CHAPTER 16

Alverton implored her with his gaze, wishing she would close the distance between them. She was so near her breath clouded, joining with his own. He simultaneously wished to pull her close, while his rational mind scolded his impropriety.

He felt his heart tug as she stepped back, lowering her gaze as though she deemed herself unworthy of him. Her expression clouded, while his grew as clear as the icicles hanging from the barren tree branches at the edge of the grove.

He'd been blinded earlier by her deceit and he had been unable to see her character for what it was. Once the dust settled, he could see plainly, and he felt the fool now for how he had treated her. Perhaps that was due to the stark contrast he felt when leaving her and entering the company of Miss Rowe.

Evelyn's goodness shone brighter than any flattering, coquettish *lady* of his acquaintance. It mattered not that she didn't have a title or an elite social standing. She was good. Too good to settle as a doctor's wife.

"You deserve far more than he can offer you."

"You mistake me," she said, "he has not offered. Not since…well, I am not certain he will accept my suit now, but I am determined to try."

Alverton shook his head, confused by her choice of phrasing. "I'm afraid I do not understand."

"I must not speak of it until I have had a chance to speak to *him*, your grace. Forgive me, but I must keep quiet at present." She closed her lips, her eyes shining with determination.

"Can I not persuade you to bring me into your confidence?" But even as he said the words, Alverton knew it was far too great a favor to ask.

And her silence was telling.

"Very well," he said curtly. The lack of trust stung, but he knew he was asking too much of her. "I shall relay a note to the vicarage directly and you must return to the safety of your home."

She nodded, dipping a curtsy before turning to leave.

He watched her walk away for a moment before turning toward Chesford Place.

"Your grace," Evelyn called, causing him to turn back. She was hurrying toward him, her breaths quick and shallow, and his heart leapt. "If you shall take my advice and return to London, allow me to take my leave of you now."

"I shan't go without a farewell," he promised, though he didn't know why. Before he succumbed to the temptation of calling on Mr. Trainor, he had been prepared to wash his hands of her. Part of him had wanted a glimpse of Evelyn when he visited the Trainor house, but he had told himself his purpose in calling was his interest in learning more about the man who was determined not to give up his political seat in direct consequence of his health. And he had learned a great deal.

With each successive visit, Alverton had learned more about Mr. Trainor, and more about the man's family. It was through the raw conversations and stories of Evelyn and her brothers that Alverton had begun to gather a realization that he'd been wrong to hold one mistake against Evelyn.

And speaking to her now, he drew the conclusion that he'd been correct in his growing assumption over the last few days: he'd misjudged her.

"Very good, your grace," Evelyn said. She seemed reluctant to leave and he held her gaze, trying to read the emotions there.

He watched her a moment longer, listening to the wind as it whipped around the grove and threatened to steadily worsen. He was hesitant to let her go, for a very small part of him was convinced he would never see her again.

But that was madness. And the storm *was* growing worse.

Sweeping her hand into his own, he brought it to his lips. Turning it around so he might face her palm, he bent his head and placed a kiss on the space between her glove and her sleeve, on the exposed skin. Alverton heard her breath catch and his chest swelled in success.

This beautiful, unaffected woman had captured his attention and he was prepared to tell her to forget Dr. Cooper and run away with him just then. But his mouth would not open to speak the words that his kiss had implied, and his hand dropped hers. Fear spread through him at the reaction he was sure to garner from his mother, grandmother, and Society as a whole were he to announce a connection with Miss Trainor, a woman of no status worth mentioning.

He squeezed his eyes closed and counted to ten to clear his mind.

It was as though magic was at play, however, for when he opened his eyes once more, Evelyn was gone.

※

MOTHER TRAILED behind him as Alverton pulled on his riding boots and snatched his gloves from the footman.

"But I do not understand where you are going!" she cried, following him about from one place to the next as he prepared to leave. "Have you seen the storm outside? I cannot like it at all."

"Sanders has yet to return," Alverton said. Again.

"And for good reason," Mother said with feeling. "Surely he has found somewhere safe to wait out the storm in the village."

Alverton turned, piercing his mother with a glare. "I made a promise to a friend that I would have a note delivered and my conscience would not allow me to send an innocent footman into that storm." He needn't tell Mother that it was Evelyn which inspired him to have a conscience on that score. But she had. And Alverton needed to do this for her. "And besides that, Sanders is not home."

Mother groaned, dropping herself onto the chair against the wall and leaning her head back as though she was doing her best not to faint into a puddle on the floor.

"Send a footman!" Mother screeched, then pointed. "There's one right there. He should do nicely."

Alverton did not bother to respond. It was only days ago that he would have agreed with her—the servants were paid for this very thing. But he knew how Evelyn would frown were he to do such a thing, and he could not bring himself to act in any way that might incite her displeasure. He could not ask the footman to risk his life when Alverton was just as capable. It was he who made the promise to have the note delivered, and he who would accomplish this goal.

"It is decided and I will not hear another word of it."

Alverton crossed the room, ignoring his mother's exaggerated sniffles, and swung the door open.

The wind and snow which blew in as he opened the door caused him to question his sanity. But regardless of his growing moral sense, he could not leave Sanders out in the storm.

He could only hope that his mother was correct and Sanders had found a place to wait out the terrible weather. But Alverton knew it was not the case. Something in the very depth of his gut knew that Sanders was in trouble. He located the barn and accepted the reins of a prepared horse from a stable boy before he swung himself onto the frozen saddle, rubbing the steed's neck in companionship. "Let's find him," he said.

They rode away from Chesford Place, down the road which ran along the grove. Alverton swept his gaze over the ground but snow was falling so quickly that any man who might have fallen an hour ago would already be fully covered in a white blanket of powder.

His nerves heightened the further he went, and by the time Alverton reached the edge of Derham he was positive he had missed Sanders.

But he was so close to the vicarage; it would only take a moment to leave his message and then he could continue his search.

Sliding from the horse, he grabbed the reins and led the animal all the way to the door, pounding loudly on the thick wood.

A tired looking man answered the door, his clothing telling a story of his limited means. Alverton knew at once that this was the man who'd come into town searching for family and had come up empty-handed.

How would he feel were he to arrive at his mother's ancestral estate in search of his aunts and find that they relocated without so much as a letter? He would be hurt, surely. But he would also be able to stay at the nearest inn and return home forthwith. This family clearly did not have the funds for such an expense, and they did not have anywhere else to turn.

And all of this after losing their home and possessions in a fire.

A strange resolve overcame Alverton and he greeted the man, asking, "Is Mr. Hart in?"

"Yes, just this way," the man said, indicating the house.

"Perhaps you will relay my greetings, for I am eager to return home. It is you I have come to see."

His eyebrows rose but he did not speak.

"I have heard of your plight and I've come to offer you a position at Chesford Place."

"Sorry, gov. Haven't heard of it," he said apologetically.

"It is an estate just south of here with plenty of land. I am sure we can find a comfortable arrangement. The vicar will point you in the proper direction if you would come once the storm has cleared. Likewise, another home nearby can accommodate two additional servants, albeit temporarily. When you come to Chesford Place, we can direct you there as well, if there be others in your family able and old enough to work."

Hope shone in the man's eyes and it was uncomfortable for Alverton. But while he was unused to this sort of exchange, he felt a warmth in his soul which burned and grew as he watched relief fall over the man's face. Was this why Evelyn was forever serving others?

Alverton nodded briskly. "Is there an earl in there, by chance?" he asked gesturing inside.

When the man shook his head, Alverton cursed. He discovered the man's name to be Mr. Howell and bade him farewell before swinging onto his horse again and turning back for the road.

"Alverton!" a voice called from the vicarage. He glanced over his shoulder to see Sanders standing in the doorway, waving to him to stop.

Alverton turned the reins sharply and the horse responded with jerky motions. He felt the animal's back hooves slide and his stomach dropped out from under him. He could tell the moment he saw more white sky than shrubberies that he was going down, and he did not have enough time to stop it.

Air whipped around his body as the horse disconnected from him. Alverton smashed on the hard ground and black closed in around him in one swift motion.

CHAPTER 17

"Do you think the storm will let up tonight?" Evelyn asked, pushing her dinner about her plate slowly with the tines of her fork.

"I am not sure," Father responded. "It could rage all night, or it could move on swiftly. We must wait and see."

Evelyn could not seem to escape the panic which had seized her as she'd walked away from the duke earlier that afternoon. She could not place precisely why she had the feeling, but the distinct impression came to her that she might not ever see the duke again. It was madness, but it was unrelenting.

"I cannot help but think of that poor family," Evelyn said. "Can you imagine coming all the way to Derham only to find that your family had moved away quite a while ago? And after enduring a fire and losing everything."

"It is a shame, but we shall rally. For all of its small size, the people of Derham are of good stock."

Except for the Hollingsfords, of course. But that was an uncharitable thought. And in truth, Evelyn did not know them. She only knew *of* them.

The room was quiet but for Evelyn's fork and father's chewing.

Aunt Edith had taken a tray in her room and the boys dined in the nursery.

So many things had occurred of late which had come to Evelyn secondhand, whether by her brother or her aunt, and she was tired of the information passing around her. She needed Father to be straightforward with her.

"Might I ask you a question?" she said before she could lose her resolve.

Father smiled at her endearingly and she swallowed. "Are my brothers in danger of losing their inheritance?"

He stilled, which was not a good sign, the only movement on his face that of his mustache, quivering in anger. "Why do you ask such a thing?"

Evelyn chose to hold strong. "Because I need to know in what way I must prepare myself. I will not see them sent to the poorhouse, Father."

"It will not come to that," he said. "I had hoped you would make an affluent match during the Season, but your stubbornness won out, I daresay."

"Is that why you had the duke here this afternoon? A last effort to secure prominence?"

Father scoffed. His cheeks grew red and he pushed up from the table, his chair sliding backward roughly on the wooden floor. "That man came to speak to me about matters of politics, and nothing more. He has visited the house four or five times now, and never once inquired after you. I have never set my sights on a title on your behalf, and you would do well not to speak such absurdities."

Properly reproached, Evelyn dipped her head. "Yes, Father."

He likely did not hear her as he had already begun stalking from the room.

Now she *really* could not eat. Pushing her plate away from her she leaned back in the chair, expelling a breath of negative air.

She hated to admit it, but it made sense that Alverton would come to speak to her father about politics, and nothing more. The man was probably going wild with the women in attendance at Chesford Place and needed a reprieve. He most likely did not intend on running into Evelyn.

But he had. And confusing was the only word to describe their interaction. She had the express belief that he had been just as hesitant to leave her in the grove as she had been to leave him.

It mattered little, though, for she had admitted to him, essentially, that she was planning to marry another man.

Closing her eyes, Evelyn dropped her head into her hands. She needed to get a handle on her feelings. They were irrelevant where status and livelihood were concerned. Dr. Cooper might not be able to keep them all in the house they had now, but he could make her comfortable, and Father and the boys would always have a place with her.

Aunt Edith, of course, could go live with cousin Harriet. Far, far away.

With that decided, Evelyn rose from the table and took herself up to bed. Now that Father had confirmed Aunt Edith's threats about the state of their income, Evelyn was left with little choice. She would become an engaged woman by the end of the week.

※

SHE AWOKE to bright sunlight streaming through her bedroom window. Blue sky met her and a soft blanket of undisturbed snow covered the ground. The storm had cleared. A sense of urgency ran through her veins and she threw back the bedclothes, dropping her stockinged feet onto the floor and shuffling over to the bell pull.

Her maid arrived and helped her dress, putting up her hair simply. She smoothed her hands over the serviceable, brown muslin and blew out a breath of air. How had the duke ever believed her to be a lady when this was what she wore?

Oh, what did it matter?

She took herself downstairs and into the library. It was empty, but a fire burned low in the hearth. She was too uneasy to partake of breakfast, but she could not trace the source of her discomfort.

Perhaps it was merely her trouble with Dr. Cooper and the desire she had to settle things before Father returned to London after Twelfth Night. She was certain he would not press her to join him if she had already obtained a husband.

Calling for her cape and gloves, Evelyn dressed for the weather. Pausing by the door, she informed the butler of her direction and went outside. There were inches of snow, but it was not impassable. And the clouds which hung low in the sky yesterday were far gone, leaving behind a cold, crisp winter day.

She trekked slowly toward Derham. Perhaps it would have been wiser to ride a horse, but the ground was slick and she did not trust an animal above her own two feet. By the time she reached the Cooper household, she was frozen to the bone and looking forward to a bracing cup of tea and a hot fire.

Which led to immense frustration when the housekeeper answered the door and informed Evelyn that neither of the Cooper siblings were at home.

"Where might I find them?" she inquired.

"Miss Cooper is at the vicarage."

Evelyn nodded, turning for the vicarage. Julia was involved heavily with the new family in town, it would seem. Someone ought to remind her that the vicar had capable servants, as well.

Rapping her knuckles on Mr. Hart's door, Evelyn stepped back to wait.

The door swung open to reveal a housekeeper with a bustle of noise behind her.

"I've come to see Miss Cooper," Evelyn said.

The housekeeper nodded, ushering Evelyn into the vicarage. "Yes, yes. Everyone is here. It is a full house if you don't mind my saying so."

"I had heard about the unfortunate family who came—"

"No, not only them," the housekeeper said with wide eyes, her mouth forming a perfect circle. "'Twas that wretched storm. Did you not hear about the *nobility*?"

The swirling in her stomach heightened and grew. "The earl or the duke?"

"Well, both of them are *here*, of course. But only one of them is not waking up."

Julia passed by the corridor then, her arms full of a bundle of linens, a weary expression on her face. She'd donned a worn, white apron which crossed over her back and tied in a bow.

"Julia!"

The woman paused at the sound of her name unceremoniously shouted behind her. Turning back, she blew out a breath. "Evelyn, have you come to help?"

"If that is what you need from me, then yes."

"Come."

Turning back up the stairs, Julia fled. Evelyn snuck past the housekeeper in the narrow corridor and followed her friend up the stairs and into a small foyer which opened to several doors. The house was snug, but there were rooms enough to fit a family. Perhaps the vicar would one day fill them with children of his own.

Julia waited at a doorway, her hand gently pausing over the handle. "Last night was likely the most trying and pleasant night of my entire life, Evelyn." She swept her gaze over her friend's gown. "'Tis a good thing, I think, you wore that gown."

Without further explanation, Julia opened the door to reveal a woman with light, frizzy hair lying on a bed against the center of the far wall, her head bent toward a bundle swaddled in her arms. She lifted her face toward Julia and offered her a wan smile, dark circles rimming her eyes.

"The baby has come?" Evelyn asked.

The woman and Julia both looked to her. Her cheeks warmed. That had been an inane question.

"Yes," Julia nodded, crossing the room and setting her bundle of linens at the foot of the woman's bed. "And I believe we ought to change the sheets and help Mrs. Howell bathe."

Evelyn swallowed. Was this not what servants were for? She did not mind helping, but she was utterly out of her area of expertise.

"The servants," Julia said, as though she could read her friend's mind, "are all busy helping my brother and the vicar. It is an unfortunate thing."

Her eyebrows gently pulled together as she reached for the baby, smiling down at the child with a glimmer in her eye.

Evelyn began pulling her gloves off one finger at a time and set them on the chair near the door. She untied her bonnet and cape and laid them safely away before facing Julia. "Tell me how I might help."

Julia offered the baby in her arms, and Evelyn's heart raced.

"Her name is Rachel."

She accepted the tiny bundle, holding her close to her chest. Rachel's head was covered in soft, dark, downy hair and her eyes closed as she made soft mewling sounds in her sleep.

Evelyn was blind to the world as she held little Rachel, her heart swelling in love for the tiny little person who relied so heavily on others for support. Julia took care of Mrs. Howell with the help of the housekeeper and they bathed the woman, helping her into a fresh night rail and onto the newly changed bed again.

Rachel began to fuss uncomfortably, her eyebrows pulling together as her tiny rosebud lips pursed. A soft, muted crying began and her mother settled back against the headboard of her bed, holding her arms out for her child.

"She is hungry."

"And we must see if Jared has need of our help in the next room," Julia said.

Evelyn paused halfway across the room, holding the crying baby, her gaze turning sharply toward her friend. The housekeeper who was gathering soiled linens to remove from the room had mentioned earlier that a Peer was here and in trouble. Evelyn had pushed the thought from her mind when introduced to the baby, but now her body was humming with anxiety.

"Who is in the next room?"

"Who isn't?" Julia said, exasperated. "I believe it is just Jared and Lord Sanders at present."

Evelyn swallowed. "Who is ill?"

"Oh, you didn't hear?" Julia asked, looking to Evelyn with wide eyes. She dropped what she was doing and crossed the room, resting her hands on Evelyn's arms as though supporting the writhing baby she held there. "He fell from his horse yesterday and hit his head something fierce."

"Who?"

Julia swallowed visibly, her eyes concerned. "The duke."

CHAPTER 18

A muted, crying baby sounded in the far recesses of his mind and Alverton could not place, for the life of him, precisely where he was. What he could place, however, was the dull, painful throbbing at the back of his head.

His eyelids felt heavy as he tried his best to pry them open, but he did not immediately register much beyond a dark, unfamiliar room.

Soft humming sounded just above his head and he allowed his eyes to drift closed again. He was very obviously not on a feather mattress in Chesford Place, if the straw poking into his back was any indication. But he could not—for the life of him—recall how he came to be in a dim room on a straw mattress with Evelyn for company.

For who else could be humming such a soothing melody?

The last thing he remembered was foolishly kissing Evelyn's exposed wrist in a show of—what, exactly? He was uncertain what he had meant by the action, only that he had not been thinking straight. He'd convinced himself that the inferiority of her birth was irrelevant. That as a duke, he was entitled to break the rules and marry whom he chose.

But at what cost?

The humming continued, soothing his nerves. But how had they gone from the woods to a bedchamber? The throbbing at the back of his head was incessant, growing the more he tried to puzzle it out. He'd been in Sanders Grove with Evelyn, and then the storm had grown worse and worse until…

Alverton's eyes shot open, coming face to face with Evelyn's soft, green eyes.

She let out a small gasp and her hand rushed up to cover her heart. "Your grace!" she said, breathlessly.

His head ached as he tried to pull back his elbows to sit up.

"No, your grace," Evelyn said, reaching forward to push him gently back down by his shoulders.

He succumbed to her soft direction, her fingertips pressing against his thin shirt. He didn't want to admit it aloud, but lying flat was much less painful than trying to sit up.

"You must wait for Dr. Cooper to come and see to your injury before trying to move yourself."

His eyes trained on her and he registered the concern playing over her features. "What happened?" he asked.

She looked between his eyes before glancing over her shoulder. "I was not present. I can fetch—"

"No," he said quickly. "Do not send for anyone yet."

"But your grace, this is not at all proper," she said, a small degree of playfulness to her tone. There was a hint of challenge as well. "I wouldn't want to compromise you."

That was a valid concern. Alverton realized the truth of her words and shock rippled through him at his own carelessness. But what surprised him even further was the very distinct fact that he was not at all worried about Evelyn forcing him into a marriage to save her own name. He had the express feeling that if *she* was put into such a position, she would not require that of him.

But he would want it, all the same.

Surprise filled his very soul as he watched Evelyn fidget with the hideous embroidery on her brown gown. She was so unassuming. So kind and generous. She was willing to risk her life in that wretched snowstorm just to relay a message that she would do her best to help complete strangers.

And Alverton loved her for it. It never would have occurred to him to serve another person in such a way, he would have simply sent a servant. But he could see how the service Evelyn rendered others brightened her soul, and it touched his heart. Much as it had when he'd spoken to Mr. Howell earlier.

"Please tell me," he said, his voice hoarse from disuse.

Evelyn rose, crossing to the ewer on the other side of the room, pouring a glass of water for him. She handed him the glass, guiding her hand in between his shoulder blades to help him sit up just enough to drink.

"Very well," she agreed. "Do you not remember the fall?"

"That is not what I meant, Evelyn. I want you to tell me that you haven't—"

"He is awake?" a deep voice said from the door, garnering Evelyn's attention.

Well, he could not inquire *now*.

"Yes," Evelyn answered. "Only just. I've given him some water."

Dr. Cooper nodded, letting himself into the room. "I apologize for leaving you. I can take it from here if you'd like to go."

Evelyn's gaze traveled to Alverton, uncertainty in her eyes. "I would be happy to stay and help."

"If you insist," Dr. Cooper said, a little edge to his voice. "But I am sure the duke would appreciate privacy for his examination."

A pretty blush spread over Evelyn's pale cheeks and she dipped in a curtsy before walking from the room.

Dr. Cooper watched her go and Alverton realized that the man did, indeed, care for her. Hadn't she mentioned she did not know if the doctor would accept her suit? It was such an odd prospect that Alverton could not be certain what she had meant at the time.

"What happened?" Alverton asked.

"Your horse slipped. You went down and he fell on top of you. You do not remember?" Dr. Cooper asked, his eyebrows drawing together.

Alverton searched the corners of his mind. He did remember riding to Derham and speaking to the man about the job, but then he had left.

"Oh," he said, remembering the white wall of snow and turning back when his name was called. "Yes. It is foggy, but I recall bits of it."

"That is not unusual," Dr. Cooper said, stepping close to peer into the duke's eyes. "It will come back to you in time, I am sure. You hit your head on the ground. You were fortunate not to hit any rocks, or we could be having an entirely different conversation, but the icy ground was bad enough."

"Will this blasted headache ever leave?"

"Eventually, I suppose. Head injuries are nothing if not mysterious."

"That is what I feared," Alverton muttered.

Dr. Cooper completed his examination. "You must be careful with what you consume today until we know how your body reacts to food. I asked Hart's cook to prepare broth and I'll have it sent up right away. Is there anything else you would like?"

"Yes. I should like to get out of the vicarage. Can you send for my carriage?"

"Might we wait until you have eaten, your grace? I would advise you give yourself a couple of hours, at least. It is not uncommon for head injuries to manifest in…well, suffice it to say that it is very likely you will cast up your accounts."

"Well that certainly explains the swirling in my stomach." He had wondered if that was due to Evelyn's humming. But no, this was more than excitement. It was nausea.

The doctor left the room, pulling the drapes tighter on his way out.

Alverton filled his lungs, expelling the breath slowly. He heard a growing chatter of female voices downstairs that grew louder as the maid opened the door to bring him a tray. He was pleased to find that Evelyn followed the maid inside and tried his best to offer her a smile.

"Is there anything I can get for you, your grace?" she asked. "Or anything you'd like me to send for?"

"What is the commotion downstairs?" he asked.

She looked guilty, her glaze flicking away. "Your female relations have come to inquire after you, but Dr. Cooper will not allow them upstairs."

Alverton's eyebrows rose. He promptly winced and lowered them.

Evelyn came around to the head of the bed with two additional pillows and helped him to sit up so she could place the padding behind him. He was not upright, but he was angled enough to make eating less of a chore. Evelyn took the tray from the maid and set it over his lap.

Taking her previous seat angled near the head of his bed, she watched him closely.

It did not escape his notice that the maid claimed a chair alongside the wall.

Evelyn must have noticed his gaze, for she said, "Alice remained by my side for the duration of my shift sitting with you, your grace. She had been gone but a moment when you awoke."

"Did you hum while she was in the room, as well?"

A blush spread over her cheeks as she glanced to the maid. "No. You heard that?"

"I am sure it was your humming which caused me to wake."

Evelyn shook her head but a small smile graced her lips and he wanted to see it grow.

"You must eat, your grace. But Dr. Cooper asked me to remind you to take it slowly."

Alverton speared her with a gaze. He lifted the spoon to his lips and drank, the warm broth soothing his body as her humming had calmed his mind.

"I am in earnest," he said.

"You are too much, your grace," Evelyn said, rising.

Alverton's hand shot out and grabbed hers. He swallowed another spoonful of broth and said, "No, stay."

Her gaze was frightened but he firmly held on until she sat again. Slipping her fingers from his own, she glanced to the maid who sat against the wall, her face trained toward the floor.

"Will you sing for me?" he requested, though he knew what her answer would be.

The small, playful smile she shot him was worth it, though. "No, your grace. Now please eat more soup."

"Yes, my lady."

"You must not call me that," she admonished, a severe expression moving over her face.

"Have you agreed to marry the doctor?" he asked.

She averted her gaze. He watched her, setting down his spoon. Why put off a declaration when he was so sure of his own feelings?

Reaching for her hand, he took her delicate fingers in his own. "Oh Evelyn, how could you consider marrying anyone but me?"

Her eyes darted to his. "You must be jesting."

"No, I am in earnest. I am prepared to speak to your father and arrange an agreeable settlement. I want you to be my wife."

CHAPTER 19

Was he in earnest?

His face looked pained, but his eyes implored her. He lay on the bed in nothing but his shirtsleeves, and she did her best to avert her gaze from his very open neck.

She swallowed, pulling her fingers from his warm grip. "I cannot believe anything you say in this state, your grace. You hit your head rather hard yesterday."

"Headache or not, I know my own mind."

"But *I* cannot know it, and I will not trust that which is said under such trying circumstances. You've only just awoken, your grace."

His altered state of mind could not be trusted. Her thoughts traveled back to the kiss he'd placed on her wrist while they were in the woods, and she stood, wringing her hands. It was all too confusing, and she needed to get away from his stifling influence.

"I will leave you now, your grace."

"Wait," he said, reaching for her again. She swiftly stepped outside of his reach.

"Good day, your grace. I will pray for your healing."

Evelyn closed the door softly behind her, her mind shooting back to the moment when the duke had called her *my lady*. Though he spoke it as though it was her title, he emphasized the *my* in such a way that Evelyn's heart had flipped over in her chest. She was prepared to admit that the man had a place within her heart, but they were not compatible. How could she accept a man who sustained a head injury just the evening before offering for her?

Though, she owed him credit in the growth of his character. He seemed a changed man since the moment she caught him speaking to her father in the library. The fact alone that he was willing to condescend to talk politics with a man who served in the Commons was enough evidence of that.

Carrying Alverton's tray down the stairs to deliver to the kitchen, Evelyn turned the corner to find Dr. Cooper standing in the corridor, leaning against the wall with his head dropped low.

"Sir?" she asked, gathering his attention.

He turned toward her slowly, his face grim.

"What is it?" she pressed. There was a sorrow about his eyes that ripped through her very heart. She longed to rush forward and soothe her friend, but the tray sat between them and she had nowhere to set it down.

"'Tis nothing," he said, offering a grim smile. "Merely a lonely man's reverie. Never mind me."

Something within her told Evelyn that the trouble Dr. Cooper faced had nothing to do with health of the body—but perhaps he suffered health of the heart.

And she could pull him from his misery with her plan to marry him. It was the smartest course of action available to her. She had determined to follow it—to inquire with this man whether he was still interested in marrying her as he had claimed to be before she left for London. His own sister requested that Evelyn not toy with his heart. Was that not proof enough he was unchanged?

But her mouth remained closed. She could not convince it to open no matter how many times she ran the logic through her mind. Alverton's odd and very recent proposal sat like a wall between her objective and taking action, and she stalled, helplessly.

"Allow me to take that," he finally said, reaching for the tray.

Shrill voices trailed into the corridor from the closed door at the end of the hall and Evelyn winced.

"The duke's family is in the parlor," Dr. Cooper explained. "I have told them they are not to bother him while his headache remains, for we do not want to cause permanent damage."

A younger voice—the cousin, no doubt—whined obnoxiously just then and Dr. Cooper shared a small smile with Evelyn.

"That would not be good for the duke's health, I fear," she agreed.

Dipping his head, Dr. Cooper turned to go.

Evelyn watched him retreat, her mind running anxiously. Should she follow him? What would occur if she blurted the words aloud *now*?

The door opened to the parlor and Mr. Hart stood in a halo of light.

"Ah, Miss Trainor. Do come in," he said, a pleasant smile on his face. She could not escape the connection now and felt Dr. Cooper slip away before she stepped into the room.

The vicar introduced her to the duchess, Mrs. Rowe, and Miss Rowe. Julia sat unobtrusively in a chair opposite the women, and Evelyn immediately chose a seat near her friend.

Julia looked exhausted. Her smile lacked its usual pleasure, and dark circles formed under her eyes. Her lack of rest the evening before was apparent in her wan expression and her consistent yawns. Evelyn wanted to find a way to encourage her friend to go home and sleep, but with such elite company she found she couldn't think of what to say.

"My poor Alverton," Miss Rowe said, raising a handkerchief to dab at her eye.

Well, that certainly garnered Evelyn's attention. What would the young woman think if she learned that *her poor Alverton* had proposed to Evelyn just moments ago?

Sniffling, the young woman continued. "I cannot think of him lying ill without my heart breaking into pieces."

"He will heal," the duchess said, her nose tipped up and a pinched mouth that reminded Evelyn very much of Aunt Edith. "The doctor said he has already awoken."

Irritation crossed Miss Rowe's brow. "Then I do not understand why we cannot see him. A simple peek to settle my discomfort could not harm him, surely."

"That would hardly be appropriate," Mrs. Rowe snapped, her gaze darting to the vicar.

"I believe he will be able to travel home shortly," Julia said kindly. "My brother merely wants to be certain that a carriage ride will not do more damage to the duke, and then he will settle the arrangements for the duke's transportation."

The women stared at her with identical expressions of confusion and annoyance. The duchess looked down her long nose, her beady eyes searching Julia up and down and finding, most likely, every thread out of place.

Julia snapped her mouth closed, her cheeks glowing pink.

Miss Rowe sighed. "This room is hardly comforting and I cannot sit here while Alverton lies in a room just upstairs. It is too much to be borne." Wailing slightly, the young woman dabbed at her eyes again. Turning soft, tearful eyes on her mother, she said, "Perhaps we would do better to wait in the comfort of Chesford's drawing room, Mama."

"Yes," the duchess said crisply, glancing about the vicar's humble parlor with poorly concealed disdain. "Let us go."

They rose and Mr. Hart reached for one of his canes, settling it before him to push himself to his feet. Julia rose as well, crossing to Mr. Hart and laying a hand on his arm as she bent to speak to him in a soft, muted tone. He looked up at her, nodding once, and lowered himself, casting a sheepish smile toward the women.

"I would be happy to see you out," Julia said calmly, clasping her hands lightly before her.

Evelyn rose, curtsying to the women as they filed from the small room. She shared an exasperated look with the vicar and wondered if *he* had managed to get any sleep last night.

It was not an appropriate question to ask, however, so she kept her mouth closed.

"At this rate I should begin charging. I could have been a fantastic innkeeper," the vicar said wryly.

"Your charity has not gone unnoticed," Evelyn replied. "And I know you shall find blessings because of it."

He turned his gaze toward the open doorway. "I am hopeful," he said quietly.

Julia came back into the room, sharing a look with Mr. Hart before dropping onto the chair beside Evelyn with dainty grace.

"All the way to their carriage they could be heard lamenting the lack of respect. Well, I never!" She scoffed. "They can take their lack of respect and—"

"Julia," Evelyn said, stopping her friend. "Perhaps I might walk you home?"

Turning to face Evelyn, her cheeks rosy from an oncoming blush, Julia nodded. "That would perhaps be best." She glanced to the vicar, her eyebrows pulling together in concern. "Should I remain, sir? I do not want to leave you with too much of a burden."

"You may go, Miss Cooper. I have servants enough to handle the remaining guests."

They took their leave of the vicar and Evelyn accepted her gloves, cape and bonnet from a maid who'd retrieved them from upstairs. They seemed to do little, however, for cold seeped through her clothing and cooled her skin the moment she stepped outside.

"That must have been a mad house yesterday," Evelyn said, drawing her friend's hand around her arm.

"I would be satisfied if I never have to endure such a night again. Jared was traveling back and forth between the duke and the laboring mother all evening, Mr. Hart was unable to assist and quite downtrodden about it, and Lord Sanders merely sat in the duke's room and moped. To mention nothing of the Howell children."

"Lord Sanders?"

"Indeed. He sat by his friend's side all night waiting for the man to wake. He only left just before you arrived—and he took Mr. Howell and the children with him. The saint of a Lord has agreed to lease them a cottage on his property and will find them positions within his estate. At least for the eldest daughters and Mr. Howell. The others are far too young."

"What kindness," Evelyn breathed. "If all of nobility could have such warm hearts, there would be a wealth of sorrow relieved."

"Yes," Julia said, sighing. "But we must be content in knowing that while *some* people of affluence are quick to turn their backs on those in need, others will do what they can to assist."

Indeed. The Hollingsfords had it within their authority to help but had chosen not to.

Much like she would have expected from Alverton at one time. But his presence at the vicarage was telling. Had he chosen to go himself to deliver her note instead of sending a servant in the storm?

"I have every hope of marrying such a fine man, myself," Julia said softly.

"And you shall," Evelyn said.

Julia cast her a look. "Perhaps sooner than you realize."

"Who is the man?" Evelyn asked, pausing in the lane.

Julia shook her head. "I cannot say. Yet."

"You will leave me in such suspense?"

Julia cast her an apologetic look. "I have made a promise, Evelyn. But I will speak to you the moment things are settled, I vow."

Evelyn sighed dramatically. "Very well. I shall not press you further. But do tell me if I am to be happy for you?"

Julia's eyebrows pulled together. "Of course."

A smile settled on Evelyn's lips and warmed her heart. Before she had left for London there had been many conversations between the friends lamenting Julia's lack of suitors and fear of remaining a spinster. Had the Earl of Sanders made Julia an offer? Or perhaps another worthy gentleman?

"I shall sleep soundly until the assemblies," Julia said as they reached her front doorstep.

"If only the same could be said for your brother." Evelyn indicated Dr. Cooper crossing the street further down. He appeared as though he could drop to the ground at any moment and fall into a deep sleep, and yet he crossed from the vicarage to a street which led to the Taylor's house, and Evelyn assumed he was doing his duty to check on his patients.

Julia nodded. "If only he can find someone."

"Who's to say he won't?"

Julia pierced her with a look. "He will not even bother looking while his eyes are fastened so securely upon one woman."

Evelyn swallowed. It was on the tip of her tongue to inform her friend of her plan to accept him, but the words would not leave her mouth. Instead she said, "It is not intentional."

"I know," Julia said, sighing. "Good day, Evelyn."

Turning from her friend, she picked her way across the cobblestone street to the road which led toward home. Her thoughts were wrapped up in the events which had transpired since the storm set in, as though the snowy clouds had brought trouble with them. She was glad things were settled for the Howell family, and that Dr. Cooper expected the duke to make a full recovery. What she could not remove from her mind was her own personal dilemma, and the safety and future of her brothers.

"Good day, Miss Trainor."

She glanced up from her reverie and found Lord Sanders sitting atop a horse not far from her, his hat removed as he nodded to her.

"Good day, my lord."

"Quite a storm we had, was it not?"

"Indeed. I have just come from the vicarage. It seems that quite a few people were affected by the weather."

"Alverton is set to make a full recovery," he said.

She nodded.

"Shall I extend your greetings?"

"You needn't bother, my lord," Evelyn said. "I extended them myself."

Sander's brow rose. "And yet, his own mother was not permitted in the sick room. They've just returned to Chesford and Miss Rowe was positively distraught over not laying eyes on the duke."

Evelyn could not contain her smile. "I believe Dr. Cooper thought it would benefit the patient's health to keep loud noises away from him until his head has healed properly."

"Wise man."

"He is," Evelyn agreed.

Lord Sanders regarded her closely, his eyes narrowing slightly. "And here I wondered…" He shook his head and closed his mouth. "Well, I must be off. Good day to you, Miss Trainor."

Dipping a curtsy, she watched his horse trot away.

CHAPTER 20

*D*r. Cooper was satisfied by Alverton's progress and deemed him fit for a short ride home that evening. He was fortunate, he'd been told, that he'd only acquired a bump on the head and nothing more. But an injury which caused him to be out of commission for an entire night was nothing to take lightly, and the doctor requested Alverton do little more than rest for the next fortnight while he checked on him daily.

Alverton wondered if such extreme measures were necessary. But he promised to listen for the first few days, at least.

Sanders sent for Alverton's own carriage and helped him outside. The walking was manageable, but his head pounded fiercely and by the time he was settled against the plush squab he was ready to sleep once again.

"I was fortunate to encounter Miss Trainor this afternoon," Sanders said as the carriage rumbled slowly down the lane. "I would not be surprised if we were to hear an announcement of her engagement shortly."

"What causes you to say that?" Alverton asked, his eyes closed.

"Nothing in particular. But the way she referred to the doctor today caused me to wonder about the nature of their relationship."

Alverton's eyes shot open. Sanders was watching him.

"You know you must act now or you could very well be too late," he said, shocking the duke.

"What do you mean?" Alverton asked, though he could guess.

Sanders shook his head. "I am no fool. I have seen where your affections lie. I cannot claim to know Miss Trainor, but I can see that she is far better suited to be your wife than that wretched Miss Rowe."

"Miss Rowe never had a chance."

"And you might miss yours with Miss Trainor if you do not act quickly. The doctor has been in love with her for years, according to the servants' gossip. And she clearly returns a level of his regard. People have married for less."

"Gads, Sanders. Is this really the time?" Alverton's head pounded and his body felt weak. He already offered for her once that day and was quickly dismissed. He needed to sleep for a week and then he would be able to address the issue of Miss Trainor and the doctor. To argue his case.

"I overheard the doctor speaking to the vicar last night when you were asleep, which was why I questioned the servants at all," Sanders said, unrelenting. "Cooper seems to feel that you are a threat to his suit and has chosen to make one last effort to secure her hand before you are able to do it first. The vicar seemed to think Dr. Cooper did not have much competition."

"Because Miss Trainor would never accept me?" Alverton asked. He swallowed a laugh at the pathetic truth to that statement.

"No," Sanders said. "Because you are too proud to offer for her."

Alverton shut his eyes again. The vicar was an astute man. Alverton indeed suffered from pride. A fault which caused him to push Miss Trainor away initially and forbid himself from considering her a valuable partner. But the vicar did not realize one thing.

He did not realize that Alverton *loved* Evelyn. And love trumped pride. Or that the duke had foolishly mentioned marriage to the woman already.

"What shall I do?" Alverton asked, his voice soft and strained. He couldn't fault Evelyn's original dismissal. He *had* just awoken after a head injury when he'd begged her to accept him.

Sanders chuckled. "That is for you to decide. But whatever it is, you must act quickly."

He considered the conversation with her by his sick bed, when he'd asked her to sing and she'd merely laughed. The woman cared for him, or so he'd let himself believe. But she could not believe his suit to be authentic. How did he alter that? "She does not take me seriously."

"Then prove to her you mean it."

That, he could do. If only his head would cease its pounding long enough to determine a plan. "Stop the carriage."

"I did not mean now—"

"Stop the carriage," Alverton repeated. "Direct your man to drive to Miss Trainor's house now."

Sanders watched the duke with trepidation. He opened his mouth to argue once more but must have realized the sincerity of Alverton's request, for he pounded his fist hard upon the ceiling and waited while the carriage rolled to a slow stop.

When the servant arrived at the door and heard Sanders' request, he did well not to look surprised. "Right away, my lord," he said, after flicking a glance in the duke's direction.

The carriage pulled slightly forward before it began turning around and it was clear that they had already reached Chesford Place—Sanders' home.

"Would you like to remain here while I go about my errand?" Alverton inquired.

"No," Sanders said at once, a grin forming on his lips. "I would like to watch this unfold."

The remainder of the ride back to the road and then onto Evelyn's house was silent and Alverton grew anxious. The feeling could not be good for his healing.

"Perhaps this was not the best time," Sanders began, warily surveying his friend.

"No, you said the words yourself. I must beat Cooper to it."

When the carriage stopped once more, Alverton pulled himself up and out of the carriage, his head throbbing as he picked his way toward the front door, Sanders remaining behind. A footman had gone on ahead of him and as he mounted the stairs and entered the foyer, the butler stood in wait.

"Miss Trainor, please," he said unceremoniously.

The butler nodded. "Might I direct you to the parlor, your grace?"

"Is it empty?"

If that shocked the butler, he did not show it. "No, your grace. Mrs. Chadwick is settled in the parlor with Miss Trainor."

"Then the library?" Alverton asked.

"Yes, that is empty, your grace."

He grunted, wishing he could fall into bed. But first, he needed to beg Evelyn to become his wife. Again.

The butler led him toward the library and he sat on the end of the leather sofa, waiting with as much patience as he could muster.

"Your grace," Evelyn breathed, and he raised his head to find her standing beside the door, shocked. "You should be resting. At home."

"I have all night to rest. I needed to see you. Please, come in."

An amused smile lit her lips and she acquiesced, coming to sit across from him in a large, overstuffed chair which positively dwarfed her.

Silence stretched as he consumed the sight of her. Regal and poised, yet kind and warm. She was duchess material and he had been a fool to ever think otherwise. The only thing he would change were her hideous gowns—she deserved to be clothed in the very best.

"I owe you an apology," he began. "I have been prideful and arrogant, and I did not see sense that day in the grove."

She appeared as though she agreed with him, though she was too much a lady to say so aloud. Funny, that.

He cleared his throat. "I realize I may be shocking you with my forwardness, but I could not go one day further without knowing you forgive me for the way I reacted to your admission."

"Of course I forgive you, your grace," she said without delay.

"Then must you sit so far away?"

Her eyebrows rose and her gaze shot to the open door. Standing, she crossed the blue carpet and lowered herself on the other end of the sofa.

"Evelyn," he said, reaching for her hand. "Please tell me you have not received another offer of marriage. Please tell me I am not too late."

The quiet between them grew and stretched until the chatter in another room further down the corridor could be heard. He began to grow anxious waiting for her to speak.

She finally opened her mouth and said, "I cannot, your grace. For it would not be true. I received another offer of marriage just this afternoon."

CHAPTER 21

Alverton looked as though he was a child and his mother had come along and taken away his new puppy. It tore through Evelyn's heart to see him so disposed, but she feared it was inevitable.

For she could never be a duchess.

"What do you mean?" he asked.

"Precisely that. Another gentleman called on me not a half hour ago and requested that I marry him."

He swallowed visibly. "And what did you answer the man?"

She sucked in a breath. "That I needed to marry."

Alverton squeezed his eyes closed and dropped his head. "I shall leave you," he said, pushing himself to a stand.

She yearned to explain the whole of it, but the dowager duchess came to mind and she promptly closed her mouth again. How could she follow in such esteemed footsteps? The woman had hardly spared her a glance upon meeting her in the vicar's parlor earlier that day; surely she would never permit a union between Evelyn and Alverton.

Even if he chose to defy his mother, what sort of life would that be? Evelyn would not wish to cause discord between them.

But Alverton's mother aside, Evelyn knew her own mind quite well. And her daydreams of childhood and the desire she held onto for years of becoming a lady of nobility and prestige were not, after all, the desires of her heart. She was far better suited to being the wife of a doctor in a small country parish, than a duchess. "Allow me to escort you out," Evelyn said, reaching for his arm and supporting him.

He pulled away as though her touch had bitten him. "No, I can walk. Good evening, Miss Trainor."

He bowed, but the wince on his brow was evidence of his discomfort. She watched in sorrow as the duke left her alone in the library, taking himself from the house with no triumph. He'd intended to ask her to marry him *again*, of that she had no doubt. But he was not in his right mind, and the moment his head healed from his trauma he would undoubtedly regret his decision.

Evelyn blew out a huff of air. Was he positively mad? The man had come into her humble house with the direct knowledge that she was a simple daughter of a gentleman with the express interest in making her a duchess.

Regret began to form in her stomach, but she quickly squashed it away. Her feelings aside, it felt wrong. She felt as though she'd swindled the man into falling in love with her. He did not love Evelyn. He loved the idea that Lady Eve had planted in his mind. He was smitten by her voice, true, but also by the dream she had created when she led him to believe that she existed as a lady.

And it simply wasn't true.

She would do much better to accept Dr. Cooper and live a cozy existence in the squished house in Derham as a doctor's wife.

She could excel in that capacity. She did not even know what to do were she to become a duchess. And then, to be under the tutelage of Alverton's mother? She wrinkled her nose in disgust. It could not be borne.

"Evelyn," Aunt Edith said crisply, her mouth pinched in disdain. "What did the duke speak to you about?"

"He inquired about my evening," she said truthfully. "I told him of Dr. Cooper's visit."

Aunt Edith watched her through hawk's eyes and Evelyn's skin crawled.

"You better make a choice quickly," the older woman said. "Security is a valuable thing."

Security for Evelyn, or for her family? She watched her aunt a moment longer. "I will do what is best for my family," she said. Of course she would.

Aunt Edith grunted before leaving the room, her heels clicking down the marble floor.

Evelyn squeezed her eyes closed and leaned back against the sofa.

"For what it's worth," a small voice said behind her, causing her to jump up. "I rather like the duke."

She turned around to find two sets of eyes watching her beneath unruly mops of red hair, tucked underneath the writing table along the far wall.

"Harry and Jack, I have told you many times how terribly rude it is to spy on people. How long have you been there?"

They pulled themselves from their hiding place, sheepishly dipping their heads. Harry's leg was doing much better, and his limp was less pronounced than it had been the day before. The gash was healing along quickly and they had Dr. Cooper to thank.

And Alverton, she realized, as she considered his part in carrying the boy all the way from the grove.

She focused her attention on her younger brothers, doing her best to appear stern. "Well?"

"We were here first," Jack said.

Harry added, "And we didn't *try* to listen."

"Off to bed with you both."

They groaned, their voices joining to create one irritated sound.

She raised her eyebrows, holding her expression as they trudged toward the door.

Jack looked back over his shoulder as he reached the corridor. "The duke is really nice."

She wanted to groan, but resisted. "Goodnight, boys."

"Goodnight, Evelyn," they chorused back.

Now she simply needed to determine *how* she ought to inform the doctor that she would be his wife, when the very thought sent her stomach into swirls.

※

"This cannot be a good idea," Evelyn whispered as their carriage pulled away from the house. Darkness met her outside the windows and she trailed a gloved hand down the foggy glass.

"Whatever can you mean?" Aunt Edith asked, her feather bobbing along with the bouncing carriage. "It is merely an assembly."

"But I look ridiculous," Evelyn argued. She should not have allowed Aunt Edith to persuade her to wear the violet silk, but she *did* believe it set off her eyes rather nicely and the gauzy overlay had eventually won her over.

Her pride had allowed her to dress in such a way. But what would Alverton think?

She shook her head. He was not going to be there. Not with his injuries. And in any case, her objective of the evening was to let Dr. Cooper know she had decided to accept him.

"You do not look ridiculous. Those ugly brown gowns you constantly wear look far sillier than this."

"Than my cousin Harriet's cast-off? It is a fashion from three years ago, at least." Not that Evelyn minded the out-of-date gown. She was merely fretful.

Aunt Edith snorted. "Be glad she married so well or she would not have left those gowns behind for you to benefit from."

Evelyn turned, facing the window. She was grateful, of course. But she did not have to rejoice in the cast-offs, did she?

They pulled in front of the assembly hall, halting in the center of the road. A servant opened the door and let down the step before handing out each of the women. Evelyn turned toward the assembly hall, light spilling from the windows onto the street and highlighting Derham society within.

Aunt Edith gripped her forearm, forcing her to spin back around and face her irritable aunt. Evelyn attempted to yank her arm free, but the older woman would not relent. "This is possibly your last chance to do anything you can to snag a titled husband. Do not be foolish, girl. You are much too exalted in your opinion of yourself. You owe it to your father and your brothers to do what you can to secure their safety and happiness."

Evelyn held the woman's gaze. While her advice was ill-formed, her reasoning was sound.

"I have a plan," Evelyn said calmly. She did not inform the woman that her plan involved a doctor and not a duke or an earl, but that was irrelevant. That she did what she could to provide for her family was uppermost in her mind.

Aunt Edith released her and Evelyn pulled back, rubbing her arm. She kept calm composure as she formulated a new plan to convince her brothers to place a frog under her aunt's pillow when the snow melted and the amphibians returned.

"Let us go in."

Evelyn entered the room after her aunt; her heart beat rapidly as she laid eyes upon Julia and Dr. Cooper standing just off to the side of the room. It was time. She had promised the doctor when he'd called on her that night, renewing his offer, that he could expect an answer by Twelfth Night. Which meant she only had a few hours left to accept him.

Her stomach churned as she crossed the room toward her friend, her smile slipping between nerves and joy. How could she go through with this when the very idea set her body to shaking? She adored Jared Cooper; he was a good man. But he was not Alverton.

And blast her wretched heart, she'd fallen in love with the duke.

Pausing in the middle of the room, she heard the voice she'd thought of constantly over the previous week. Turning slightly, she first caught sight of the over-frilly debutante cousin of his, flanked on either side by regal, turban-endowed matrons of poise and distinction. How Alverton ever convinced the women in his family to attend the assembly was shocking, and Evelyn wished very much to know of his method.

That the man himself attended just one week after falling from a horse was an absolute miracle.

She paused, her eye catching Alverton's and her world sliding to a halt. He watched her over the crowd of people gathering to dance, and she found she could not avert her gaze, so securely was he holding it in his own.

"You look breathtaking, Miss Trainor," Dr. Cooper said just behind her. Evelyn turned to face him and her stomach sank at the hopeful look shining in his soft, blue eyes.

Suddenly, she knew she could not accept him.

How could she live with herself if she agreed to marry a man who cared so wholly for her when her heart was pinned on another man?

Jared Cooper deserved better than that.

Evelyn would have to return to London with her father and secure another husband, but that was the cost. It would be easier to endure an equally loveless marriage than one so painfully unbalanced.

His hand reached for her and he asked, "May I have the pleasure of the first set?"

Dipping her head in acquiescence, Evelyn placed her gloved hand within his own and followed the doctor to the center of the room to line up beside the other couples. She did her best to deliver a pleasant smile to her partner but was afraid she simply looked pained.

Glancing over Dr. Cooper's shoulder, she caught the duke's eye as he leaned against the wall. A blush warmed her cheeks—so pointed was his attention—and she was grateful when the music began.

What message was he attempting to send to her? She'd already rejected his offer of marriage. Surely he would return to London the moment he felt he could withstand the trip.

Had he come merely to torment her?

"You appear quite distracted this evening," Dr. Cooper said.

"Forgive me," Evelyn said. "My mind refuses to rest."

The dance began and she felt Alverton and Dr. Cooper both watching her with equal interest, one man from his place standing beside the wall, and the other while he danced with her. She was overwhelmed, the stuffy heat of the room causing her corseted stomach to draw quick, shallow breaths while she tried to dance gracefully in the unfamiliar gown.

"Might I be so bold as to request sitting out during the next dance?" Dr. Cooper said. "Or would you prefer to dance?"

She looked down the aisle of couples and found Julia partnering Lord Sanders. Her friend's smile was beautiful, her hair arranged more intricately than usual. Was that in an attempt to impress the earl?

Bringing her attention back to her partner, she said, "That would be fine, Dr. Cooper."

The conversation needed to occur whether she wanted it to or not. It was just as well that she should put the man from his misery sooner rather than later.

They danced the remainder of the song with little conversation but the energy humming between them was fraught with nerves.

"Have you spoken with Julia yet this evening?" he inquired.

"No," Evelyn said. "But she is positively glowing."

"Indeed," he agreed. "My sister has cause for such joy. I think you will find her well pleased."

Evelyn searched the dancers for Julia's face and found her friend at once. Julia's countenance was bright, her smile unrelenting. "You cannot force me to wait to learn the nature of that joy, Dr. Cooper. Not now."

He smiled softly, finding his sister in the crowd before saying, "She has agreed to marry Mr. Hart."

The vicar? Evelyn nearly missed a step due to her surprise, but a quick glance at Mr. Hart seated along the wall was enough to prove Dr. Cooper's claim. The vicar watched Julia with a contented smile, his eyes glimmering with joy. Evelyn found her heart lightened with happiness for her friend, for clearly, Julia was delighted with the arrangement.

As their dance came to a close, Evelyn dipped into a curtsy, doing her best to avoid Alverton's strong gaze watching her from across the room. She placed her hand on Dr. Cooper's forearm. "Might we find somewhere more private to speak?" she asked.

He agreed, leading her to the door. The back of her neck warmed and she followed him, her heart racing as she tried to determine how best to let him down.

"I can only assume," he said finally, as he led her to a secluded bench just outside the assembly hall, "that you do not have good news to share with me."

She glanced up sharply. "Why ever do you say that?"

"Because you cannot seem to look me in the eye," he said softly.

Her cheeks grew warm and she cast her eyes to her hands, watching her fingers fidget. "I cannot marry you, Dr. Cooper."

He sighed. "I figured so."

She lifted her chin, doing her best to hold his gaze. "It would be unfair to you. I cannot accept you when my heart belongs to someone else." Drawing a breath, Evelyn continued, the words resonating and settling as she said them. "I could not marry you for the sole purpose of security and comfort. It does not rest well within my soul."

His lips formed a small smile. "And I could not sway you if I promised that I do not mind if you married me for the sole purpose of security and comfort? I believe we could find happiness."

"You are probably correct, but I cannot take such a chance. And I cannot sit here any longer and allow you to guard yourself from the possibility of loving another woman."

He stepped forward, reaching for her hand. "But I am content loving *you,* Evelyn. I am happy to do so for the rest of my life with the mere hope that you will grow to return my regard in time."

And she could, potentially, reach a level of contentedness herself. But she did not love him in that way. And she was quite afraid she never would. "But what if I cannot? Dr. Cooper, please accept my refusal."

"Very well," he said, releasing her hand. He glanced back to the assemblies. "I believe our dance is coming to a close. Might I escort you back to your aunt?"

"You needn't," she replied. "I can find her well enough on my own."

He nodded, his hands grasping behind his back. "If it is all the same to you, I believe I will take my leave."

She dipped her head and watched him walk away, his shoulders bent in defeat. It sorrowed her that she couldn't accept the man, but it was for the best. Now she needed to find a way to explain that to Julia.

Letting herself back into the ballroom, Evelyn sought out Lord Sanders and Julia within the dancers. The song was indeed drawing to a close and she had promised the next set to the earl.

"Might I claim the next?" Alverton asked, coming to stand beside her. He was dashing in a well-cut navy coat, his cravat starched and flawlessly falling into his waistcoat.

Her body hummed anxiously at the duke's proximity but she did her best to appear unaffected. "I am sorry, your grace," she said, continuing to search the crowd, "but it is promised to Lord Sanders."

"He will not mind."

She shot a glance at the duke, amused to find him standing beside her, watching the dancers without a care in the world. "You are confident, your grace."

He speared her with a look. "I hope I have every right to be."

Where was this coming from? The last she'd spoken to him was days ago in her father's library after he'd been injured, and he had left the room with solemn acceptance. That was quite different from the attitude he was affecting now.

Lord Sanders escorted Julia to a seat along the wall beside the vicar—Evelyn assumed Mr. Hart to have claimed the next set—before turning toward Evelyn and the duke. The couple smiled at one another, love exuding from each of them and Evelyn wondered how she had not seen the connection herself earlier. Julia was going to make a perfect vicar's wife.

Lord Sanders reached them shortly and bowed. "I believe this is my set."

"Unless you are willing to forfeit it to me," Alverton said. "I would be much obliged."

Sanders turned toward his friend, his eyebrows lifting. "What has the lady to say of this arrangement?"

Evelyn was at a loss. She'd never been placed in this position before. It could not be proper.

"If Miss Trainor has no objections, I would be happy to oblige," Sanders continued, "but I will gladly hold my honor and dance with her if she finds the arrangement distasteful."

Evelyn swallowed. "I do not find it distasteful, my lord."

He stepped back, flourishing his hands toward Alverton. "Then by all means, please excuse me."

Alverton reached forward and Evelyn placed her hand on his arm as he led her to the floor. A soft, slow instrumental began and Evelyn found her heart beating rapidly within her chest.

"Dr. Cooper has gone home, I take it?" Alverton asked, his voice low.

She nodded, turning away from him in the motion of the dance. When they came back together, Alverton said, "And might I be so bold as to inquire *why* he chose to leave the Twelfth Night ball before midnight?"

"He found much to be disappointed in, and little to entice him to remain."

"You rejected him," he said plainly.

"Yes," she answered with equal frankness. "I could not marry a man who loves me so dearly when I do not return his regard. The imbalance would cause me to resent him in time, I fear."

The dance continued, bringing Evelyn and Alverton together several times in close proximity. The longer their silence stretched, the more shallow Evelyn's breathing became, until she could no longer look the duke in the eye without fear of suddenly swooning.

Evelyn was too strong a woman to swoon; the idea bothered her very much.

She trained her gaze upon the buttons of the duke's gold waistcoat instead.

"Shall we remove ourselves from the room at the close of the dance?" Alverton asked.

"No, thank you, your grace. I have done as much this evening once already and the experience was far from enjoyable." If she could remain within the busy ballroom until Aunt Edith was prepared to return home, then she would be safe from reliving the earlier rejection.

"I would like to think a conversation with me might have a more favorable outcome," he said, his deep timbre washing over her.

"Why ever do you think that?" she asked. She might love the man, but that did not mean she was any more suited to marry him.

"Because I have learned a few things and I am quite certain you would like to know them as well."

Drat the man. Why had he fed into her curiosity? It was unfair. "Still, I cannot think it is wise. I would prefer to dance."

"Fine. We shall dance."

The song came to a close and the master of ceremonies announced the minuet. Alverton led Evelyn to her place and took his own, watching her while they waited for the song to begin.

When the first strains of the violin cut through the air, Alverton leaned forward. "Please listen carefully, for I fully intend to convince you to agree to become my wife."

CHAPTER 22

Her eyes were wide in shock, and Alverton had to guide her through the first few steps before she regained her bearings. He cleared his throat, prepared to argue his case.

When her young brothers had come to his house earlier that day with their insights and stolen information, he had been skeptical at first, but so far they had proved accurate: Dr. Cooper had not received an acceptance a week prior like Evelyn had allowed Alverton to believe.

"I have been put under strict authority not to reveal my sources," he began, further garnering her interest, he hoped, "but I was told that you have been falsely informed of the dire straits of your father's finances."

She paused, widening her eyes. "How can you know of that?" she whispered loudly, her gaze flicking to the surrounding dancers.

"Are you prepared to meet me in private now?" he asked.

She looked unconvinced.

"I promise not to press you," he said. "I merely wish to talk."

They could not leave the dance now without ruining the set. Instead, they moved through the motions together, Alverton's stomach growing more nervous as the dance neared its close.

As the final strands of the violin sounded, Alverton bowed,

reaching for Evelyn's hand. He caught sight of Miss Rowe standing beside her mother, watching him closely, but he ignored the irritating girl.

She'd done her best to visit him within his own chamber on three occasions that week and he'd informed his own mother that if they were not removed from the house by the end of the day tomorrow then he would forcibly remove them himself. He was through putting up with the dowager's antics.

"This way," he said, releasing her hand. It would not do for them to be seen leaving in such a way. He stepped through the door and she followed. He led her into a parlor just through the inn on the other side of the wall, and she looked ill at ease.

"Perhaps we ought to go outside," she said. "I am sure everyone in that hall watched us leave."

"I will be quick," he replied. "Your aunt has lied to you. Your father is not in dire straits, and your brothers will not be sent to the poorhouse. You could remain unmarried for the rest of your days and comfortably reside within your own house, if your brother permitted it after he inherited."

"How do you know such a thing?"

"My informant overheard your aunt speaking the falsehoods and investigated the situation. I am not ashamed to say that I questioned your father myself when I learned of this so I could be certain I was delivering accurate information to you."

"When?" she asked.

"This afternoon," he said. "After my little informants told me everything, I was fortunate to receive a visit from your father. He has taken to visiting me this last week while I laid in my sickbed, and I learned a good deal about your family and situation between our political conversations. He had no trouble trusting me with this knowledge today when I asked him to verify the claims."

She stared at him and Alverton did his best to smile easily. He lowered himself on a chair and indicated the seat opposite him. Evelyn sat, her dainty eyebrows pulled together in confusion.

"We are not poor?" she asked softly.

"No."

"Then why must I wear those wretched dresses?"

Alverton chuckled. "I did not inquire on that score, but my assumption is that the discrepancy is found in your father's lack of knowledge or interest in ladies fashion, not the lack of funds."

She chuckled, bewildered, leaning back a little in her chair. "How did I not see that before? I did question him about Aunt Edith's allegations, but he was so focused on my insult that he likely missed the intent of the conversation."

"Suffice it to say, you need not marry simply to protect yourself or your family. Your aunt lied to push you into a union, no doubt."

She shook her head. "It is not very shocking, you must understand. On our way here tonight she attempted to convince me to snag a title while I still could."

"Then let us move on to more pleasant matters," he said, standing. He crossed the rug and sat in the chair beside hers. Her face remained calm and composed, but her eyes widened infinitesimally. "I was also able to learn through these anonymous informants that when Dr. Cooper came to the house before me and offered for you, you did not answer him right away. But you let me believe you had."

"I wanted you to leave me be," she said, wincing. "Forgive me, your grace, but it is the truth. I could never accept you and I needed you to understand and return to London so I might sort out my life in peace."

He tried not to feel hurt by her rejection. How had he ever thought she had tried to snare him? It was madness. "Why could you never accept me?"

"I am *nothing* like Miss Rowe," she said with feeling. "Furthermore, I was not raised to take on a role with such a grand title or distinction and I would not know what to do or how to act. I could never reach the grace your mother exudes." She sighed, resigned. "It is too great a duty to bear, and one I was not born to. If I was meant to take on the role, then God would have seen fit to place me in a position to learn it. As it is, I am content with my lot in life."

"What utter rot."

"Your grace!" she gasped, her cheeks growing pink.

"Excuse my language, but I heartily disagree. I have spent my life being told of my superiority. I believed I was better than everyone else for so long that I'd lost the opportunity to be the man I ought to be. You've shown me through your generosity and kindness that the rank does not make up the person, but the *heart* does. And you have the heart of a duchess."

She shook her head, so he reached forward and lifted her chin. "Miss Rowe is not suited to the position. She merely wishes for the esteem. I have spent years rejecting the women you described, and I had no idea that who I needed was living in a small country house in the middle of Wiltshire." He smiled, unable to contain his amusement.

"But how would I face your mother if we wed? The *ton*?"

He took a breath and asked a question which both excited and terrified him. "Do you love me?"

She paused, gasping. Seconds ticked by and he did not remove his gaze from her, anguished by each moment she had yet to respond. He sucked in a breath and said, "Because I love you, Evelyn. Most ardently."

※

How could she respond to such a declaration? She could see the sincerity in his eyes and wanted his reasoning to resonate within her, but the truth remained; she was frightened.

Swallowing, she leaned back out of his grasp and his hand dropped onto his lap.

"I love you," he reiterated. "And I am willing to stand by your side. Do you love me?"

Evelyn considered the man sitting across from her and the earnest hope he exuded. Despite her fears, she could not lie to him. Not ever again.

"Yes," she said quietly.

A smile broke out on his lips and he stood, reaching for her hand. She allowed him to pull her to a stand.

"I believe," he said firmly, "that together, we can do anything. I took it upon myself to ask your father for his blessing today and he has granted it, but he was quick to inform me that the final decision is yours."

She chuckled. "Yes, that sounds like my father."

"He is a capable man," Alverton said. "I know you've suffered with your fears of his health, but I have a solid understanding of what ails him and it cannot be fixed by remaining at home while parliament continues to work."

Her breath caught and she swallowed. "What is it that ails him?"

"Loneliness," he said. "He loved your mother dearly, apparently, and while you and your brothers have done much to ease his life, parliament fills the void by giving him purpose."

It was a sound theory, and Evelyn could see the truth to his words. "But he relies so heavily on his cane and falls asleep constantly."

"And both of those are due to his age, and not an illness. It is perfectly ordinary behavior."

A blush warmed her cheeks. It all made sense now. Poor Dr. Cooper must have thought her mad when she begged him to evaluate her perfectly healthy, aging father.

"Now, enough of that business," Alverton said, his voice low and husky as he drew her closer. "We love one another, and all of the other nonsense has been addressed, so *please*, darling, will you agree to be my wife?"

She appreciated that he called her his wife, and not his duchess, for it was not the title which drew her to Alverton, but the man himself. And that man was a powerful, warm, gentleman. If he stood by her side, could she do it? Could she take on an impossible task and make it possible with Alverton's help?

Sucking in a breath, Evelyn leaped across her uncertainties and doubts, landing within the sphere of Alverton's support. "Yes," she said at last. "I will marry you."

He grinned, pulling her close. His hands came behind her back and she could feel the smile on his lips as he bent to kiss her. Bringing her hands up to his chest, she enjoyed the butterflies which flapped around her stomach, and the safety she felt within his arms.

When he lightened his grip on her, pulling away, she lifted her face to his. "I think marriage should be quite agreeable."

"I believe," he said, bending to place a kiss on her nose, "you are correct. Now cease your talking and allow me to kiss you again."

And she did.

EPILOGUE

TWELFTH NIGHT, FIVE YEARS LATER

Pulling the gathered boughs from the bannister, Evelyn dropped them one by one onto the pile gathering on the floor below her. They had the rest of the following day to clean up the decorations, but with two children sick with colds they had been forced to cancel their celebration and Evelyn was determined to clean the dried-up boughs so that her hands were free to slide down the smooth railing once more.

"You needn't do that, you know," Alverton said, descending the stairs with an amused smile on his lips. "The servants shall take care of it tomorrow."

"My hands wished for something to do." She leaned her arm against the smooth, bough-free railing and tilted her head back to look at him. "How are the children?"

"Julia is asleep and her maid has been instructed to watch her closely. Alexander has determined he is not sick, for he wishes to ride his new pony tomorrow."

"Is that true?"

"No," Alverton said, clearly amused by his son's antics. "He's heating up. But I promised I would take him outside the moment his cold subsides."

Evelyn huffed. "There is nothing so miserable as a sick child."

"At least they've only contracted colds. They shall be up to running about the corridors in a day or two, I'm certain."

"So we should appreciate the quiet while we have it?"

"Yes," Alverton said, stepping down the stairs until he reached her. "Come with me. I've something to show you."

She took his hand and followed him from the room and to an archway that led to the drawing room. He stood in the center of the archway, slipping his hands around her waist.

"What is it?" Evelyn asked.

"Well, my first surprise is that my mother has determined not to leave London yet, for she doesn't think she can withstand the cold and wishes to remain with my grandmother."

Relief washed through Evelyn. She had grown to love her mother-in-law, but she was quite pleased to be left in peace as well. "And your second surprise?"

"That your father shall arrive within the week with Harry and Jack for a visit. He can only stay a day or two, but the boys shall remain until they are needed back at school."

"Oh, darling, that is splendid news!"

Alverton lowered his voice, pulling her closer. "And it gets better, yet."

"Oh?" she asked, wondering how her heart could grow any more full than it already was.

"Yes. Look up."

She did and found a small sprig of mistletoe tied with a red ribbon attached to the archway above them. A smile slid onto her lips. "And is that my third surprise?" she asked.

"No," he said, bending toward her. "This one is mine."

She fit perfectly in his arms and sighed, contented. "I love you, darling."

"And I love you," he said.

And then the duke bent down and kissed his duchess.

OTHER BOOKS IN THE BELLES OF
CHRISTMAS SERIES

*Can be read in any order

Unmasking Lady Caroline by Mindy Burbidge Strunk

Goodwill for the Gentleman by Martha Keyes

The Earl's Mistletoe Match by Ashtyn Newbold

Nine Ladies Dancing by Deborah M Hathaway

ABOUT THE AUTHOR

Kasey Stockton is a staunch lover of all things romantic. She doesn't discriminate between genres and enjoys a wide variety of happily ever afters. Drawn to the Regency period at a young age when gifted a copy of *Sense and Sensibility* by her grandmother, Kasey initially began writing Regency romances. She has since written in a variety of genres, but all of her titles fall under sweet romance. A native of northern California, she now resides in Texas with her own prince charming and their three children. When not reading, writing, or binge-watching chick flicks, she enjoys running, cutting hair, and anything chocolate.

Made in United States
Orlando, FL
06 May 2023